T.C.A. Srinivasa Raghavan is an award-winning financial journalist who also writes on politics and economic history. He has also written short stories. This is his first, and last, attempt at full-length fiction.

Goodbye to All That

A Delhi Story

T.C.A. SRINIVASA RAGHAVAN

SPEAKING
TIGER

SPEAKING TIGER PUBLISHING PVT. LTD
4381/4, Ansari Road, Daryaganj
New Delhi 110002

Published in India by Speaking Tiger in paperback 2018

ISBN: 978-93-88326-38-4
eISBN: 978-93-88070-05-8

10 9 8 7 6 5 4 3 2 1

Typeset in Garamond Premier Pro by SURYA, New Delhi
Printed at Gopsons Papers Ltd

To Poto, my late lab.

1

Nothing, they say, focuses the mind as clearly as the prospect of a hanging. But the prospect of a sacking from your first job must surely be a close second. I faced this in the summer of 1979. More accurately, I was threatened with a suspended sentence. I had recently been told that I had a year to find three five-star authors for my publishing list, or else...

I had gone over my likely fate at least a hundred times since it was first proposed two weeks earlier by the Englishman. He had said it in the circumlocutory way that is so typically English. But the message itself was stark: shape up or ship out.

I was the commissioning editor for economics for a large British publisher's India operation. I was twenty-nine. I had been at it for four years and eight months. All in all I had done a pretty fair job. Or so I thought. In fact, this had been reflected in successive annual reviews as well as the accompanying increments in salary which, I have no hesitation in saying, were very generous. I had been able to live in the style I had been accustomed to all my life.

But here I was being told to do better or pack up.

The most unfair part was that it wasn't my fault. My bosses knew it. Their bosses in London also knew it. But the way it all worked, there was nothing anyone could do about it. You played on the wicket they gave you.

We were a top class publishing house and as such should have had no difficulty in attracting top class economists to publish with us. But we didn't. This was because, as always with the British, there was a chicanery problem. London took away the best writers from us because it operated on the principle that finders were not always keepers unless it was London who had done the finding. They owned the shop and they had first dibs on everything. In the last two years they had taken away five of the best and the brightest from my list. Their books had shown up in India as imports from London.

It was not a formal rule. It wasn't even a convention. Nevertheless it was there. In essence therefore, I had been asked to compete with London. It was, I had told the managing editor, like asking a ten-year-old to face the West Indian pace quartet and make some runs. Oddly enough, however, although the ultimatum should have worried me a lot more, it didn't.

I knew chance played a large part in these things and that eventually it would work in my favour, too. The question, though, was whether it would within the next twelve months. Star authors were hard to come by because of the way stardom was defined. It had less to do with the contents of a book and more to do with the success of the author's efforts at networking in the academic community.

I woke from my latest contemplation of the future when the car went over a large bump or perhaps pothole, you could never be sure. Mike, Shiv, Debbie and I were driving through a thick dust storm of the North Indian plains, through western Uttar Pradesh generally, or just beyond Meerut, precisely.

Debbie, an English medical student, had never seen anything like it, not even in Upper Volta where she had gone as a volunteer the previous year. She didn't show it but I think she was very nervous. The sky was dark with the dust. We couldn't see more than a few feet ahead. The wind was fierce. The car was an old Standard Herald. And we were still about 150 kilometres away from Dehra Doon, our destination, to attend the wedding of my closest friend.

Debbie had turned up at my door two days previously after a phone call from the railway station. 'I am the friend of a friend of Sunidhi,' she had said. 'She said I could stay for a few days with you.' Sunidhi was my ex so I had invited Debbie over.

She was tall, about five feet ten inches, and well-built. The sort, I later thought, that had helped build the Empire and not, like the later Mems, just live off it. I couldn't see her coming out with the Fishing Fleet looking for a husband. Nor, in the unlikely event she did, could I see her going back to England without one.

She was wearing an olive-green battledress, a sort of smock or something, the type English nurses are shown wearing in field hospitals in those dreary desert war films. She had cut her hair very short, almost a crew cut. She had blue eyes, brown hair and, on the whole, a very pleasant countenance. Only her very dirty Hawai chappals were a distraction. She saw me looking at them and went red with embarrassment.

The four of us were on our way to Dehra Doon to attend the wedding of my closest friend, Gibbsy, a Welsh Presbyterian tribal from the Northeast. His great-grandfather, like many others from his tribe, had taken on the name because he liked the sound of it. Gibbsy told me once that one of them had chosen Nuclear and another Latrine for the same reason. If names were to be rejected for their meanings, we Tamil Brahmins would not have Mahalingams, Bhoothalingams, or some other communities Kuntz and Sidebottoms.

Gibbsy had joined the Foreign Service and was marrying a mainland Punjabi whose family was from Mussoorie. Rohini, or Ro, had drifted into his life only a few months earlier. Love gradually blossomed and then the desperation to get married before Gibbsy went off on his maiden posting to some place in the Middle East. Time would tell if he could have done better, or she. But for the moment, they seemed happy.

I must say I envied them somewhat. Ecstasy caused by prolepsis lasts very briefly but it is very nice when it does. I had been there, done that and was apprehensive for Gibbsy who, despite his bravado, was a sensitive sort. He could sink into moodiness very easily, and from which he would recover only after several days. The smallest things could upset him and, over the years, I had looked out for him. And, in different ways, he had looked out for me, especially when I was finding it hard to find a decent job and needed a place to live. We had shared lodgings for over five years in, and after, college. Gibbsy was the sort who ironed his jocks and socks before putting them on. 'It used to be very cold where I grew up,' he had told me once. He said he would warm his jocks and socks over the kitchen fire because they had no electricity.

Gibbsy, like so many of his tribe, could play the guitar like a real professional. He had a finely tuned ear, very long fingers and an absolutely wonderful acoustic guitar that had a deep sonorous sound, as if it was connected to an amplifier. He couldn't sing, though. But he would insist on singing. I often wondered about how differently the same brain controlled both his vocal chords and his fingers. But as Mick Jagger sang—and Gibbsy copied atonally—you can't always get what you want.

Once during a teachers' strike in the University, he and I had gone off to Calcutta. One evening, we decided to visit Free School Street, the red light area. We went from brothel to brothel, which stank of phenyl, and just couldn't get on with it. Eventually, we went back to the flat where we were staying and drank a whole bottle of Hercules rum with egg rolls. Neither of us has ever referred to that evening since then. But once in a while we use the words the madam in one of those ghastly places used to describe us to her girls. 'Not our type.' She had said it in Bengali which Gibbsy knew perfectly because his mother was from Darjeeling. I guess we had looked what we were, scared and very wet behind the ears. Indian men grow up very slowly.

Mike was Mukhbir Singh and a pilot with Air India. Flying for him was, as Harry Belafonte once sang, like a pool of mud to a pig, a natural habitat. 'Chicks, flicks, and the very best food,' he said. 'All for doing what I like doing most, sometimes in the air.'

He had morphed into Mike in school which was one of those St Somethings that the Brits had left behind in the hill stations and other places with their mandatory complement of gays, racists and psalm singers. I had attended one such for six months in Jabalpur, going straight from six years in Delhi of *Ya kundendu tushara hara dhavala ya shubhra vastraavrita* in our 'Hindi medium' school as they were derisively called to 'Our father who art in heaven hallowed be thy name thy kingdom come', etc. I had even been caned by the headmaster for distorting the 'art'.

For no apparent reason, I had become Charlie for a while. My rechristening in Jbaps, as they called it, was done by a gang of three local ruffians called Manoj, Hansraj and Bhikhumal. But they were known as Manny, Hanny and Beeks. It was the same snobbery that turned Kamala Nagar in Delhi into KNags and Sardar Patel into Surdie Pat.

That same snobbery later made St Stephen's College of Delhi, known derisively as Mission College, into a top educational brand. Those who were undergraduates there always mention it, like the IAS chaps. It gives them status. My colleague who looked after the history list told me that this was the last but very long gasp of the Empire. 'Like a horse dying,' she said.

Mike said his genealogy could be traced back to a very sweaty union that had taken place, perhaps in the early hours of a hot and humid day in Calcutta some two hundred years ago. Keith Hobson, a lonely young lad of twenty-two from England had taken a fancy to the kindly, buxom and middle-aged Bengali ayah at his boss's house. Keith had lived for a few months above the stables. She hadn't minded his attentions because the alternative was to return to her smelly hovel in the servants' quarters where the coachman and other male help were also trying their luck. Sensibly, she had opted for clean sheets, never mind the malarial youth with halitosis, said Mike. But he never told us how he knew his forbear had bad breath.

Each night, after putting the three baba-logs of the sahib to bed, she would come over to Keith's rooms to cook the rice and fry the fish while he drank the cheap gin shipped in from England. After dinner and a quick slosh from the wooden buckets in the shed that served as a bathroom, she would slip into bed with him without bothering to dress. The inevitable happened and Keith's passion for 'doing the right thing' matched his demands of her in bed. Just before their first child was born, he married her. He died in 1800 after yet another Bengali mosquito bit him. He is buried in the Park Street cemetery, Mike told us. I had tried looking for the grave on one of my visits to Calcutta but had failed to spot it.

Keith's descendents were also not choosy about their mates. Ruling classes don't need to be because those who make the rules for others are not themselves obliged to be overly picky. My colleague, the history editor, had once regaled us with the story of how Brahmins in India made the rules and broke them all the time while forcing everyone else to follow them. For two hundred years, the Brits had been India's new Brahmins.

As a result of all that DNA crossing the only thing that remained of Keith the First was his name. It seemed an Afghan, a Burmese and a few others had helped the family along, all in proper wedlock, of course. The result in the last quarter of the twentieth century was a tall, well-built, and handsome fellow with a simple approach to life. In Mike's life, there were no grey areas.

Mike's mother was a Sikh from Patiala. Her husband, Brigadier Ravindra Singh, had been posted there when they met and fell in love. Her parents were affluent landlords who had sent her to Newnham College in Cambridge. The effects of that education had lingered on. It showed in the way she talked and in the way she saw things. She was the perfect blend of Sikh austerity and British understatedness. She had brought Mike up to be like her.

The Brigadier was not very different but since he lacked her reading, he tended to come across as man who was comfortable only with simple choices. Shades of greyness made him go very quiet and he would change the subject or get up and go for a walk in the garden. Mike was like him in that respect. But in Mike's case, as it must have been in the Brigadier's also, the overall result was irresistible to women. Mike's parents knew what their son got up to every weekend that he was in India and let him be.

When I went to their house in the Ambala cantonment for the first time, a huge army bungalow with lots of hibiscus and a couple of acres of lawn, she had shown me into a large room full of books. There had to be at least thousand there.

'Army wives lead boring lives,' she had said. 'So I read.'

During the two weeks I had stayed with them, I spent at least four hours every day in that room when Mike was asleep in the early mornings and late afternoons after lunch. I owed much of my transition from a reader of very light fiction to serious fiction and non-fiction to her.

One day, I had asked her how she moved so many books from posting to posting.

'The army is very kind,' she had said. 'They have enough people to take care of that sort of thing.'

I told her how my father, a civil servant with a fondness for reading, would discard several books on being transferred, which was once every three years. The district clubs had been the main beneficiaries.

Sometimes I wonder what has happened to that very colonial British institution. The last time I had been to a district club had been about fifteen years ago in a dusty district headquarters in eastern Madhya Pradesh. The trappings had survived almost two decades of independence and the resulting depredations of the Public Works Department. But I could see the changes that the last decade had brought.

The cane chairs on the verandahs were sagging. The china in the dining rooms was cracked. The knives and forks were not of a set. The glasses were smudgy. The khansamah and the bearers were doddering and their starched white uniforms had been replaced by personal pajamas and shirts. The white canvas shoes had given way to chappals and even bare feet. The long, dying gasps of Empire were sad but inevitable.

Then there were the circuit houses and the dak bungalows, exclusive and highly subsidized micro-sized hotels built in picturesque locations where the white officials of the Raj stayed while on tour. The circuit houses were for the higher ranks and the dak bungalows for the lower ones. They were as essential to governing India as the police and army because the Raj was run on the hoof, as it were.

The usual drill was that the sahib arrived at dusk, hot and dusty from a long day on the road—first on horseback, then in jeeps when they became available— had tea on the spacious verandah, and took a walk around the grounds, talking to the local minions like the tehsildar or patwari. These buildings could be on as much as five acres, so the strolls could last a while. The sahib then bathed, had a drink, and a simple but hot dinner. Sleep on clean sheets—and rough hairy blankets if it was winter—under a mosquito net, wake up for an early breakfast and then he was off again on the next leg of the tour.

While the circuit houses would be in district headquarters in what were called the Civil Lines, the dak bungalows were often in the middle of dense forests and you could have leopards spending the night on the verandah.

Many of these, and even some circuit houses, were without electricity until the 1960s, or without any kind of modern conveniences for that matter. They had some very strange and dark bathrooms as well. The night soil carriers were as much a part of the scene as were the masalchi and the khansamah. The latter, my father had once told us, was a source of many delectable and salacious stories about the love life of the gora sahibs who would bring along their girlfriends for an amorous weekend while the memsahib was away in England. They have since then remained a place for comfortable liaisons between male and female IAS officers who are attracted to each other.

One circuit house, set deep inside a huge compound, had huge tiger heads on the walls, even in the bedrooms, which was quite scary at night. In another, the bathroom was as big as a large drawing room in modern flats. The circuit house in Indore was massive and set on a very large estate. There was one which was perched on a small rise over the Narmada. A set of stone steps from the garden led down to the river.

Many had ghost stories attached to them. In one dak bungalow an Anglo-Indian lady committed suicide after her heart was broken by some cad of an Englishman. Then there is the story of a circuit house which was

visited by an Englishman's ghost over Christmas. He
had killed himself there out of sheer loneliness.

• • •

In due course we reached Doon. It had taken eleven
hours to cover a distance of 125 miles, the last 30 uphill.
The radiator had had to be filled five times because
of a minute leak. But, finally, there we were—grimy,
hungry and in the last stages of the strange mood of
melancholy when the ganja starts to wear out. Someone
showed us our rooms in a bungalow that had been
rented by the bride's family. Across the corridor I
caught a glimpse of Debbie unselfconsciously undressing
entirely. I had stayed there gawking and watched her
dress unselfconsciously after a shower. Lust should have
blossomed but didn't because I was still recovering
from Sunidhi's definitive departure from my life. To be
precise, she had departed and I had made it definite.
She had to feel the loss as much as I did, I thought.

    We had met five years previously, fallen instantly in
love for no reason that seemed good enough to either
of us any longer. We had more-or-less lived together
in my flat for two of those five years. Then it had all
begun to come apart, with fights, recriminations, tears,
make-up sex, all those usual things repeating themselves
with increasing frequency, until one day she simply
left, her mind switched completely off me as if she
had killed off a part of her brain. Thank god we didn't
get married, she had written to me in her last letter. I
hadn't replied. That, as they say, had been that.

Eventually, it was well past ten when two young girls came to fetch us. They took us to a huge lawn with lots of very high eucalyptus trees and very low lantana hedges. The trees were lit up with strings of lights and the hedges with diyas. The effect, despite the noise of music and chatter, was tranquil enough for the occasion. Gibbsy saw us and came over.

'No booze,' he said, answering the query in my eyes. 'But will a joint do? Good local stuff.'

So we went out of the back gate and smoked one. 'Back home,' he said, 'we do things less noisily.'

I told him about the dreary drive up to Doon and after a few minutes we went back. Gibbsy led me to a corner that had some sofas and we sat down. People were eating tiredly from trestle tables. Dry parties always end up like that, a chore and a bore, something to be got over with quickly. I wondered why the bride's family had not served some beer at least. After all it was summer and beer didn't cost all that much.

The joint took hold quietly and very differently from the ganja we had been smoking on the way up. I had told Sunidhi once that it is the difference between a decent scotch and gin, further lowering her opinion of me. Ganja, charas, etc., were on her chhee-chhee list.

I felt the telltale sense of slight languorous disembodiment creeping over me. My focus on small things began to accentuate disproportionately. The big sounds started going away while the small ones, even very small ones like the rustle of the waiters' keds-clad footsteps, became very loud and clear. I recalled how once in Gibbsy's basement flat in Timarpur I had spent an entire evening listening only to the triangle in a Dylan song. I had wondered later if Arjun, when he took aim at the fish in the reflection, had also smoked a bit before picking up his bow. My father had once told me that all those ancient sadhus in samadhis were all doped up, stoned out of their minds.

Gibbsy' mother-in-law-to-be-next-morning came up to us. She was a small but purposeful woman. She had a fully laden plate in one hand and a cigarette in the other. 'The caterers have to leave in half an hour,' she said. 'And enough charas for the night, Gibbsy, you have to be awake by ten tomorrow. The magistrate will come at eleven. He is a busy man.'

I asked a passing waiter to get us twelve puris and some mutton curry which we ate in quiet companionship, possibly our last such meal together. Mike and Shiv joined us. Someone, Debbie I think, brought some water.

'Aah,' said Mike. 'The memsahib.'

Debbie, like the few other Brits I had met till then, missed the layers of hidden meaning. The modern Brit, not having been brought up steeped in it, has no sense of the Empire. I wondered briefly if I should ask Mike to lay off Debbie but seeing she hadn't reacted, I let it pass. I was too languorous to explain anything.

The guests began drifting off disconsolately. Seeing Debbie, one of them strolled up and asked if she was English or 'any other'. She looked up in surprise. Gibbsy spoke before she could. 'Go home now, Deepak, your dog is waiting and will pee on the carpet if you don't take him out soon.' Shiv also asked the interloper to leave. Shiv's pet peeve was the Empire. His thesis, written, as he would say at Cambridge, UK—not Cambridge, MA—was on British perfidy. 'The Brits like to see their moral sores from time to time,' he said. 'It lets them get on with their deplorable and impeachable past.' Slightly built, heavily bearded and moderately bespectacled, he was a budding historian. 'Of the French Left sort, rather than the British or American variety,' he would clarify without being asked.

Sunidhi had once told me that it was a fine distinction. It rests on the idea, she explained, that morally, the French are always in the right. I had told her that if the comparator was England, that was perfectly justified and fine with me. She often cited Shiv to me, or his learning at any rate, which was quite prodigious even in college. I, in comparison, was a frivolous hedonist, she said. He had got a very nice teaching job immediately after completing his PhD but was restless because he didn't know written Urdu and Farsi, which he said were a must for him if he was to get anywhere in the profession. He worked for only around three hours every day, for five days a week. On the sixth he worked a little longer preparing his lectures for the coming week and adding bits and pieces to the book he was writing on the Ilbert Bill.

Shiv was convinced that but for that Bill, the Congress party would never have been born. The Brits ran India through a Viceroy and his council which used to have a law member. One Courtnay P. Ilbert was the law member in the early 1880s and he wrote up a law that would allow Indian judges to try white people. There was a huge outcry from the whites in India and England. They started a campaign against it. They had not forgotten 1857. Rumours were spread by the British-owned press in India that Indian judges would fill their harems with English women. The English women kept shrieking against all things Indian till the Viceroy, Lord Ripon, watered the law down. If, the revised law said, an Indian judge was trying a case against a white person, at least half the jury would have to be white. It was racism, pure and simple.

Shiv said it eventually cost the Brits their Indian empire because a few months after the law was passed, the Indian National Congress was formed. Eventually, it would inherit India from the British.

• • •

It was a wonderful evening, the air full of that peculiarly cool and sharp fragrance of the pine-covered hills. It was very silent now. The crickets were at it but that was all. We sat there quietly, three twenty-nine-year-olds, inseparable friends for twelve, each unconsciously trying to figure out how to grow up. Neither sex, nor money, both of which we had in abundance, had offered a way out. Each one of our six parents had told us that we had to 'settle' down. We wanted to but didn't know how. The mothers meant marriage, the fathers meant careers. Gibbsy had one already, and would have the other tomorrow.

'Gibbs will soon be off,' said Mike. 'To Muscat or some such place in the Middle East. No booze and girls covered from head to foot. I hate flying there.'

'The embassy chaps don't have a problem,' I told him, 'And since he will be married tomorrow, Pimms and poon-tang should be the least of his worries.' For all our dislike of the Brits we still used their slang and preferred their liquor.

Deep down, all of us knew something was ending. It was the unspoken reason why we had come up to Doon despite the heat, dust and hassle. The past had to be given a proper send-off and what better way than at a wedding?

• • •

No one woke us up the next morning so we slept till quite late. Eventually it was Debbie who did the honours. She had gone for a walk, she said, and wandered into the house where the wedding was taking place. There she had got talking to some girls, one of whom had accompanied her back with a tray loaded with two large flasks and several china cups and saucers. She was pretty in a very Delhi sort of way. Not so much the looks as the accent, if you know what I mean.

'Tea and coffee,' she had trilled—there is no other word for it—and hung around chatting with Debbie. Shiv always slept in his jocks and refused to wake up till they had left. Mike had his T-shirt on and tried to chat up the girl, who said her name was Jyoti.

'Which one of you is the pilot,' she asked.

'Me,' said Mike.

'IA or AI?'

'AI,' replied Mike.

'What's your name,' Jyoti asked.

'Mukhbir Singh Hobson but my friends call me Mike.'

'Well, Mukhbir, nice to meet you. As it happens, I also work for Air India. See you around. Breakfast is on the lawns. Debbie has eaten. I will save some for you fellows but you'd better hurry up before they close the doors.' She went off presently with Debbie.

We went through the three Ss of adult male mornings—shave, shower and the third S, though not necessarily in that order. *Sarve Bhavantu Sukhinah, Sarve Santu Nir-Aamayaah, Sarve Bhadraanni Pashyantu, Maa Kashchid-Duhkha-Bhaag-Bhavet.* That about sums up these Ss for men. Happiness and prosperity to all.

Jyoti, true to her word, had piled a table with an enormous amount of food and fresh fruits. Aloo parathas formed the backbone of the meal and from them sprang all sorts of vertebrae like kebabs, omelettes, scrambled eggs, choley, pickles, dahi, salad and a huge dish of butter chicken along with earthen cups filled with rabri.

'Left over from last night, and the better for it,' Jyoti told us. 'Tuck in and slink in,' she said pointing to the hall where the ceremony was to be held. 'Front row, four seats to the left of the aisle. Don't be late,' and went off again. I caught Mike's eye. He raised an eyebrow in silent query. I shook my head and he blew me a kiss.

Later, driving back, he told us she worked in the scheduling department, that she was a couple of years his senior in Air India, that her father was a commander who flew 747s and her mother a doctor who fixed bones, that she had a younger brother who played cricket for Delhi and, above all, that she had agreed to see a film with him after he came back from Hong Kong five days later. Mike got on easily with women but so far had never fallen in love the way I had.

'Men think they snare the women but it is the other way round,' he was fond of saying. He was probably right.

Conversation is necessary only when the taste buds sulk. We ate in focused silence that only happens when the food is absolutely marvellous. By the time we shuffled into the drawing room and sat down, it was full. A makeshift platform about two feet high had three chairs on it. There was a desk on which a Bible and a Bhagavad Gita had been placed. I assumed that the magistrate would bring the civil marriages handbook or manual or whatever it was called. I liked this absence of fuss. Civil marriages changed the agreement from a sacrament which was utterly binding, to a contract which was not. Shiv muttered to me that this was a form of western cultural imperialism.

'I wonder why the anti-imperialists have left it unchallenged,' he whispered. I had no idea what to say so let it pass.

The magistrate was ushered in by a bevy of simpering ladies who settled him into his chair. He looked about thirty and quite overwhelmed by the power vested in him. Later, over lunch, he told me he was of the 1971 batch of the Indian Administrative Service—the capo di tutti capi of the civil services of which there were a couple of dozen in India.

Gibbsy, he said, was three years his junior. 'Feels odd,' he said, 'marrying off someone who may well become my colleague a few years on.' I murmured something about officers and gentlemen and offered him a cigarette which he gladly accepted.

Gibbsy strolled in a few moments later, looking very pukka. He was exactly six feet tall and had the natural lean frame and good looks of his fellow tribals of the Northeast. His mother-in-law-to-be had chosen his clothes well, or had got someone to do it for her. The suit was cut superbly and it fell beautifully. The rich deep maroon tie served to highlight his white shirt. Colour, I have always felt, is best used only if it emphasizes the empty spaces around it. He looked down at us and grinned, a little apologetically, I thought. He shook hands with the magistrate and they started chatting.

Then Ro was brought in by her mother and aunt, father in tow. She looked a bit unsure. She had told me two weeks ago that she was getting tired of the dog-eating jokes. 'No worse than eating parmal or tinda,' I had told her. 'Tell your relatives that.' I had bought a brilliant book by Marvin Harris, the Princeton anthropologist, called *Cows, Pigs and Witches* for her.

My years with Sunidhi had improved my knowledge of sociology books, if not sociology itself which I regarded with the snootiness of an economics man. This had been another little thorn which had crept into our relationship.

Everyone then quietened down. The magistrate got up and read out from a piece of paper he took from the inner pocket of his suit and, in about twelve minutes, the ceremony was over. It would have taken even less time had Gibbsy not fluffed his lines saying 'wawfully ledded life' instead of lawfully wedded wife. Miss Ro Singh was now Mrs Ro Shilo, which was a famous name in the Northeast.

Everyone drifted off here and there, happy to enjoy the cool morning which was a far cry from the Delhi heat most of them had come from. Shiv and I went looking for a beer which we found after walking about half a mile. It was a dhaba actually, which advertised beer and momos. We drank a bottle each, felt the better for it and strolled back to the house.

By the time everyone re-assembled on the lawn it was well past noon. I saw Debbie talking to a group of elderly Punjabi men and wandered up thinking it might be necessary to rescue her but there was no need. They were all telling stories about the medical college where Debbie had been on attachment as part of her course. I moved away to interrupt Mike who was persistently getting in Jyoti's way as she went about her hostess duties.

She smiled her thanks as I drew him away to the

bar which had miraculously appeared under the huge peepul tree on the grounds. Oddly, Gibbsy's mother-in-law, who had decreed that there would be no alcohol the previous evening, had pulled out all stops now, a corner solution if there was one, I thought, the all or nothing syndrome as described by economists with maths on their minds.

'There are fewer people now, you idiot,' said Mike when I told him. That was true. There were barely fifty people to be seen, mostly relatives it seemed from the way they were lolling about. Half of them were women who did not drink during the day. There was no pretence at the formality and false bonhomie that is usually seen at weddings. Obviously, these people met frequently and felt no need to waste their breath talking. I have always found large gatherings where one is called to eat and make merry daunting because of the large numbers of strangers around. So I was glad that Mrs Singh, Ro's mother, had kept the really important event so private and intimate. If anything, it occurred to me, it was the four of us who were the strangers there.

The well-stocked bar was a help-yourself affair so Mike and I half filled three tumblers with vodka. We found Shiv and gave him his drink which he swallowed in one gulp. For some reason, he could really put away the stuff and remain mostly alright. Something to do with his metabolic rate, he claimed. Back in college, we always made him pay half the price on the grounds that he would drink half the bottle. He paid as uncomplainingly as he drank unfailingly. Mike said he drank half because he paid half but I didn't think so. It was us who drank less. Now he looked at Mike and said, 'Jyoti's getting married in September. In Delhi. At the Oberoi.'

By two thirty the lunch was determinedly over and we said goodbye to everyone. Mike looked forlorn and refused to drive. Shiv was falling asleep. So I drove with Debbie next to me on the passenger seat. Naughty thoughts fleetingly crossed my mind but there wasn't the time for anything, even if she had been amenable. She was catching the BA flight at three in the morning. It was drive down, dine out, and depart.

We talked quietly almost the entire way. We had nothing in common and should have run out of conversation in about fifteen minutes. But we didn't. And she was full of questions, which she asked through pursed lips, a habit, she was to tell me many years later, she had picked up in army boarding schools where children were not really welcome and were not expected to speak unless spoken to.

I was a great fan of Kingsley Amis who she dismissed as a 'men's' writer. She said Tom Sharpe, the comic novelist, over-wrote. She had never read Wodehouse but had heard of Jeeves. John le Carré bored her. 'You'd think there is no such thing as trust,' she said. She preferred violin sonatas to large ensemble music. Cricket for her was something England had left behind.

'It's funny how your newspapers report county cricket scores,' she said. She asked me if I had been to England. I said, yes, for three days in December the previous year, all of them at our London office, from nine in the morning to nine in the evening.

'I saw nothing and met only the two people who dealt with the India office, a fellow called Thomas Frampton and a woman called Diana Holbrooke. I arrived on a Sunday evening and left on Thursday morning. They took me to a pub one evening. That was all.'

She invited me to come again. 'The English countryside is quite beautiful,' she said. She told me her father had been in one of the Services, I forget which, and that throughout the 1960s when lots of bits and pieces of the Empire were still bobbing about, he had served there on the detritus, winding things up.

'So I didn't actually grow up in England because I went to school in all sorts of places. When I got into the medical college after Cambridge my father bought me a house and said I would have to be a landlady from henceforth and that all my expenses would have to come from the rent. It is a four-bedroom house so I have eight tenants, all students. The kitchen is common.'

She lived in the attic and shared the bathroom with two others on the second floor. 'If you come during the summer vacation, when the students go away, there will always be a room for you.' And I would not have to share the bathroom, I thought.

I fully understood her schooling experience, having gone through it myself. I told her how I too had no roots anywhere because my father, as a civil servant, had moved about all over the place. I had acquaintances but no real friends from school. Those I had acquired in college.

Last year some girls from the last but one school which I had attended for a year and half had organized a dinner. Ten years had passed and only the girls found things to talk about animatedly. The men just sat there morosely drinking Mohan Meakin's beer and Hercules rum wishing they hadn't come. I had sworn that evening never to go for any such dinner ever again.

Since then I have sometimes wondered why men drift apart so much more easily than women. I haven't found a satisfactory explanation. Once, when I asked Shiv about it, he said men had nothing but sex on their mind and saw all other men as competitors. It is as good an explanation as any.

Debbie was a good listener. She murmured questions from time to time, almost certainly because she was a stranger, whom I would probably never see again. At one point I launched into my analysis of modern Indian society and its fault lines. She sounded shocked when I said we were the bastards of Empire, brown Anglos, as it were. Brought up on Enid Blyton, Richmal Crompton, Frank Richards, Capt W.E. Johns and P.G. Wodehouse, we saw the world through a south of England prism which had ceased to exist after World War II.

'Our prejudices are those of upper-middle-class England between 1900 and 1950. As such, we tend to despise Indians who are different because they are not Westernized. We laugh at their accents, for one thing. We ignore them generally.' Yet there we were, in charge of everything and likely to remain so for a long time to come.

It was nearly nine by the time we reached home. We quickly showered, drank some whiskey and went out for dinner to the Golden Dragon near my house which had opened a few months earlier. The owner was known to my uncle so I got a discount there. Then I dropped Debbie off at the airport. She renewed her invitation to me to come to England. I said I would and bought her a book called the *Serpent and the Rope*. When I met her next, she told me she had found it unreadable.

I also dropped Shiv and Mike at their homes. We arranged to meet at my place the following weekend. Shiv and Mike both lived at 'home' and often used my flat as needed. They both had keys. Their signal to me to not come in was the 3-foot cactus left behind by the previous occupant. If it was on the gatepost, I simply turned around and left. I never asked what they did when both needed to fly the Jolly Roger at the same time. My room was put to good use, I suppose. But as they always left the flat spic and span I didn't complain.

It was nearly midnight by the time I turned in and I fell asleep almost at once. The next day was Sunday and I spent most of it in bed reading a book about old people by Kingsley Amis. Gibbsy called at around six in the evening and asked if I would like to come over for dinner. I am good at reading voices and declined. He sounded relieved.

'Right, well, leave the key out, then, will you? We will come over afterwards. Our flight is at eleven tomorrow morning.'

The two of them came around eight thirty and had breakfast. The lady who cooked for me, when she learnt they had just got married, made kheer. We sat and drank lots of tea and smoked almost a whole pack. Gibbsy always got a little jumpy before a trip, the result, he said, of having missed a train when he was a kid. He had gone to some fancy school in Darjeeling and that involved a three-day journey from Guwahati via Calcutta. He was just eight years old then, he told me. The episode had marked him forever.

Just before he left he went to the car and brought out the tiny khukri which was one of his favourite possessions. He never went anywhere without it. His father had given it to him when he was ten. It was a family heirloom of sorts, nothing very valuable but an heirloom nevertheless. He handed it over to me silently and nodded. I gave him one of my most precious books, the three volumes of the Antrobus series on diplomatic life by Lawrence Durrell.

Ro watched quietly. We shook hands and then they left. It had been as emotional a parting as any other. Invisible to Ro, perhaps, but not to Gibbsy and me.

Around noon I drove my Royal Enfield over to a theatre where I ate something and watched a film because it had Gene Hackman in it. I went back home afterwards and thought about women generally and Sunidhi especially in a jumbled way while I waited for it to turn seven.

Then I poured myself half a glass of whiskey, drank it slowly, ate and went to sleep.

2

One morning at the end of June, Mike phoned to say that his mother wanted to see me. I promised to go over that evening. They lived quite close by in Shanti Niketan at the Nanakpura end of it. I showered and changed after coming home from work and turned up at their home. It was a typical Delhi bungalow of the 1960s with a large front lawn, a big verandah, a small drive in which three cars could be parked, and a garage over which were the ubiquitous servants' quarters.

For a few months after I had got my job I had lived in one of these 'quarters' in Defence Colony. The single rooms, which were stacked one above the other, had been modified to cater to people who had just found employment. Rent was low, space was limited and coming and going was not restrictive because these 'quarters' used the old servants' entrance, usually a wrought-iron spiral staircase.

Since garages tended to be quite large, around 200 square feet, the landlords would stick a tiny bathroom and a mini-kitchen on 100 of those square feet. That left around 120 square feet for the bed-sitter which was twice the size of the rooms in college. The 'quarters' where I had stayed overlooked the drive and had huge windows. But unless you left the door open there was no cross ventilation. So that's why many people used to sleep with doors and windows open and after dipping the sheets in a bucket of water.

I could never decide if we were better off now than before when we used to sleep in the open, either in the gardens attached to peoples' houses or on the terraces. Open-air sleeping had been very common until a few years earlier. Delhi didn't have mosquitoes then but the flies more than made up for them.

Except for the four winter months, everyone slept in the open, the sahibs on their lawns or terraces and the servants wherever they could place their charpoys. Few things were better than being able to drop off to sleep gazing at the stars. Without much ambient light around, the sky would be strewn with them.

The problem was that you had to wake up at first light because if you waited for dawn, the flies would descend, forcing you to scurry indoors which would be boiling hot. Instead, everyone would be out on the verandahs in double-quick time, dozing, sipping tea and reading newspapers.

Just above me was a newly-married couple who made love practically every night and morning for the six months that I lived there. I could hear everything quite clearly, including the wife asking her husband who was a grunter not to make so much noise. They had no idea I could hear everything.

We became quite good friends after a while and

shared many Sunday lunches, with them providing the food and me the beer. He was a few years older and worked for Colgate or Coca-Cola, I forget which. She was a year younger than me and was a trainee at the *Times of India*. Had Sunidhi not walked out, they could have been us, I thought, except for one thing: she would have made sure that the door and windows were shut at the appropriate times.

• • •

Mala Auntie was sitting on the verandah which was being valiantly cooled by a noisy desert cooler placed about 15 feet away at the edge of the lawn. The grass smelt very nice because it had been freshly watered. Mala Auntie used to stick some khus reeds into the desert cooler's pads for added fragrance. These were the smells I had grown up with when my father was posted in the districts and we had lived in huge bungalows and I really enjoyed spending a few hours at Mike's home whenever it was possible.

There was a huge and ancient ivory tray on the table in front of her. It was very heavy and had belonged to her great-grandfather. On it was a full bottle of whiskey, three glasses, and a large ice bucket.

'Hello, Auntie,' I said handing her some books and half bending down, the common feet-touching gesture. Mike used to make fun of me but I think Mala Auntie vaguely approved of the tradition.

I watched her as she took them out and read the jacket blurbs. She was in her mid-fifties, slightly built and her hair had begun to grey. She had the assurance of persons of her class and education. You don't see it very often these days, that indefinable quality which automatically receives deference from everyone. Sunidhi used to call it feudal authority and disapproved of it, quite overlooking the fact that even though she was thirty years younger, she was exactly the same.

For the past twelve years she had been a sort of mother-cum-guide to me. I went to see her and the Brigadier at least once a month and often twice. She liked riding pillion on my Bullet, a heavy motorcycle still being made in India thirty years after the first one was produced in England.

Once in a while, on the Saturdays when the quarterly stock-taking was on, I would take her on it to the godowns where our books were stored. We would go after lunch. By then the books that were to be remaindered would have been counted, noted and put to one side. As a member of the staff I could buy them below even the remaindered price which itself was virtually free. Many of my colleagues would be there and it was quite good fun buying literally dozens of books, most of them in good condition. It was all read-and-throw because the covers had been ripped off. It was, I suppose, what channel surfing is on TV. I saved a lot of money on gifts as a result.

'I have this one,' she said handing me one of the books. 'I asked Mukhbir to read it but you know how he is.'

She waved at the drinks. 'Help yourself. Ravi will soon be here. He is taking a shower after tennis.'

We chatted for a bit and then she told me why she had summoned me. 'I have written a book,' she said. 'It is handwritten. Can you get it typed for me, please?'

I nodded and said I would. But before I could ask her more about it the Brigadier arrived dressed in his one of his two dozen or so shorts and T-shirts. 'He wears only these after he retired,' Mala Auntie had told me once. She had also told me that he regarded her as an eccentric for reading all or most of the time.

'Imagine what he will say if he finds out I also write,' she had added wryly.

I had wondered about that at the time but had let it go thinking it was nothing more than sarcasm. Remembering that remark, I decided not to ask her what the book was about. There was no point in starting the Brigadier off on the pointlessness of reading and therefore writing books.

Instead, I gave the Brigadier a drink, half a glass of army issue whiskey called Black Knight, and the rest ice. He took a few large sips and sighed in total contentment. My father does that too, or used to, before his diabetes was detected. Now he merely sighs with longing, to no avail usually. It was just as well that my parents lived 500 miles away. My mother was able to bully him better.

We sat silently for a while. There was no need for small talk. Over the years, I had spent so much time in their home that I was now part of the family. It was very different from my parents' home which could be bewilderingly disorderly. Mala Auntie kept a neat house, everything just so. Shiv said he found it daunting and Mike rebelled by keeping his room very cluttered. But I found the order very calming and loved to go there. My own flat was like that. I used to hate when my parents visited because within a few hours the place would start to resemble their home.

Mala Auntie finished whatever she was drinking and went in to supervise dinner. The Brigadier, by now two-thirds of the way down his glass, said Mike would be in any moment. Sure enough, a few minutes later we heard his car which he parked and came over. He poured himself a large drink and went in.

'Flying VIPs is worse than flying pigs,' he said as he went.

I asked Mike when he had flown pigs.

'Once,' he said. 'It was a training flight. I had no idea they needed so much attention, the pigs, I mean.'

It turned out that a minister had delayed the flight from London because he was shopping. Then after boarding he had got drunk very quickly. 'Even before we had crossed the Channel, would you believe it?' Mike said. Then he had pawed the senior stewardess who had complained to the captain. Mike was sent to deal with the 'situation'. The minister had then threatened him with dismissal.

'I managed to calm him down,' said Mike. 'I slipped a sleeping pill into his Chivas double. When we woke him up before landing he asked for the book and wrote nice things about me. He said he had a very refreshing nap. He slept for six hours.'

'Where did you get the pill?' Mala Auntie asked.

I told her that pilots sometimes carried a supply to help with jet lag. She didn't look very happy but said nothing. Instead, she asked me if I would like the bottle of scotch that Mike had brought from the duty-free a few days earlier, which the Brigadier was refusing to touch. The Brigadier, a lifelong Old Monk man, had switched to whiskey only after the doctors had persuaded him to. But it had to be Indian whiskey. Scotch, he thought, was for the faint-hearted. I thanked her and said yes.

We sat around for a while after dinner and then I got up to leave. Mala Auntie asked me to wait while she fetched the bottle and I did so astride my bike. She gave me the duty-free bag with the bottle and the manuscript in it. I placed it on the fuel tank before me and drove slowly home through the dark streets of RK Puram, keeping a lookout out for stray dogs. I had once come off the bike after hitting one and had no intention of a repeat. The pain from scraped skin and bruised bones had been horrible. Worse, I had been bike-less for almost a month, and broke after its repair bill came in. I never, ever wanted to travel by bus or auto again. My mother had bought me a second-hand car, an old Hindustan 14 that was built like a tank. But I didn't enjoy driving it.

It was barely ten thirty as I turned into the slip road that led to my ground-floor flat and I knew I would not fall asleep till much later. I was running out of books to read and the one I had started that morning was not very good. My mood was beginning to dip as I got closer home.

When I got there, I found the front door ajar, the lights, fan and desert cooler on and Shiv stretched out on the sofa reading something. He was drinking from a full glass of whiskey, a nice enough one called Lord Jim. That was the agreement between us. Mike and Shiv had to make sure that I was never out of whiskey because that was the one thing—other than running out of books to read—which threw me off balance. The books thing had been there since I started reading novels. But the whiskey thing was a post-Sunidhi development. After two years of coming back home to her in the evenings, whiskey was turning out to be a good substitute.

I put the duty-free bag on the dining table, went to my bedroom, showered, changed into my shorts and white sleeveless vest, sat down opposite Shiv and looked at him. He responded to my unspoken question.

'That damned woman,' he said. 'She's been at it again.'

'It' was the stealing of his ideas for research grants and presenting them as hers. 'It' had happened twice so far. The first time, Shiv said, could have been a coincidence. The second time was suspicious. But a third time? He was raging now, quietly, because unlike Mike he was not given to raising his voice. Mike almost never got angry but when he did he could be most embarrassing.

After about half an hour or so Shiv stood up to go

home. He had an early class the next day. It was almost midnight and if he didn't get a taxi or auto he would have to sleep over at my place.

'I am going to confront her and complain to the vice-chancellor,' he said.

I told him to be careful because not only was she senior to him and powerful as well, she could always send him a notice for defamation via her lawyer husband.

'Best not to discuss your ideas with anyone till you have sent in your research project,' I told him. 'And if you must do something, start a whispering campaign against her and wait for others to embellish the rumours.'

I was used to these complaints not just from Shiv but also from authors who often claimed that the referee had incorporated their key idea into his or her own book. Often, this was just a plaintive howl after being turned down but I must admit it happened from time to time because the entire game was set up that way.

When a manuscript came to me, I had to first decide whether it was worth investing time and money in. I was the first barrier. Then, if I felt it was worth a second opinion, I had to send it off to an expert in the field. This was where the problem arose because, by definition, the expert could have a conflict of interest with anyone working in the same broad area, especially if he or she was writing a book on the same or similar topic. All that was needed was to delay sending the review report, incorporate some of the ideas in the manuscript into his or her own and then write back saying that the manuscript was fine except it needed very extensive changes.

If the writer agreed, it would take him or her at least six months if not more by which time the referee's own book or paper would be out. If not, then the whole process would start again with some other publisher with the same end result. More often than not, the victims were the younger lot like Shiv who had to produce ideas and papers and books to get ahead and who would inevitably be reviewed by seniors who were past it. It was unfair, unjust and unethical. But that's how it was.

I had complained bitterly once to a professor who had taught mathematical logic in college. I had gone to ask him to referee a manuscript and started grumbling as he pottered around looking for his Charms. 'Oh, it is like Moore's Paradox,' he said. 'Everyone knows it is happening but no one will believe that it is. It is more comforting to pretend.'

Policemen, he said, often faced a variant of the same problem: they knew the accused had done it but could not prove it. In a few months, I would realize how frustrating and rewarding that could be.

• • •

Unlike most people, I had never much looked forward to weekends and post-Sunidhi, I had begun to actively detest them. It was far better, I had told my boss many times, to let me take any two days of the week off rather than insisting on my taking only Saturdays and Sundays off along with the others. I said it made no sense to stop working for two whole and consecutive days when it was far more energizing to take a day's break in the middle or even four half days a week. But she would not agree.

'There will be nothing for you to do without the others being present too,' she said.

'But most people work in silos,' I said.

'I don't,' she replied. That was two years ago and I had stopped trying after that. I would turn up at the office on Wednesdays, hang about for a while and then take the rest of the day off. I used to make up by going in for half a day on Saturdays. No one ever caught on, or so I thought till one day, quite out of the blue, she said she knew what I was up to. But she didn't tell me to stop. 'Just stay in till after lunch on Wednesdays,' she said.

Her name was Nikhila or Nikki, as we all called her. She was the managing editor and getting a bit long in the tooth but very successful professionally. She was authoritative without being dominating or domineering. She had a clear business sense which is what had got her the post when it came to choosing between her and a couple of others who were otherwise just as good. She could also be very charming when the occasion demanded, as when trying to convince the brick-headed marketing director about budgets and so on. She wasn't very much older than me, maybe forty, and very attractive in the way some women can be. She was of average height, starting to fill out nicely and clearly in her prime. The slight greying at the temples suited her.

She had been in publishing for nearly two decades and was a 'force', everyone said. She had taken her doctorate from Oxford in sociology and was very keen that we develop a strong Indian list in it. But good manuscripts were hard to come by, which annoyed her no end.

'Sociology is not just about caste,' she would grumble from time to time at the editorial meetings. She would then tell us about the harm M.N. Srinivas had done to Indian sociology. 'It was a great insight then but now we think it is the only insight worth investigating.'

I was vaguely aware of a new subject called socio-economics. I used to see books on the lists of American publishers. The British didn't seem very excited by it, so our very British company didn't bother with it. I had mentioned the new subject to her once or twice and she had told me to see if I could find any Indians working on the topic. But nothing had come of it because the economists looked down on sociology and the sociologists thought economists were clueless about people and how they behaved.

Nikki liked to meet everyone formally once a week. This was at the weekly review meetings which were held on Monday afternoons at two thirty. The idea was to see what had happened, what was going on, what ought to happen and why something that should have happened had not. The five editors, along with the production controller and a minion from marketing, attended the review. The pecking order was by seniority and not the importance of the list. I had thirty books on my list but being the junior-most had to wait my turn. It came by about four forty-five when everyone was looking to escape. Depending on how I was feeling, dyspeptic or kindly, I would take a lot or very little time over it. The simplest ploy if I wanted to delay was to ask Nikki for help.

She was very susceptible to praise and I usually manipulated her by asking, 'I really don't know how to proceed with this one, Nikki. Can you help me, please?' That was guaranteed to add fifteen minutes of experiences, advice and opinion because Nikki took her job seriously.

Another trick was to explain in detail the situation on each of the thirty titles. It was easy to consume an hour that way. One of the other editors had suggested a separate meeting just for me but had been turned down on the perfectly sensible grounds that everyone needed to know, at least broadly.

'Suppose someone quits suddenly?' Nikki had asked when the idea had been mooted.

In fact, that is what had happened not once, not twice, but thrice. My predecessor, who had become the stuff of legend in the office, had emptied a dustbin on Nikki's desk before stomping off the job. By the time I joined seven months and two editors later, one thousand seven hundred pages of final proofs were waiting to be okayed, twenty-seven manuscripts were waiting to be read, and three hundred and sixty-three letters had to be replied to. I took the manuscripts home in an auto to read at leisure. The letters acknowledging their receipt had already been sent by the boss. So the authors, poor devils, could now only wait.

The proofs were a bigger problem. I read about a hundred pages and decided this was not for me. So I made a deal with the chief proofreader, a rogue if there ever was one, who offered to do them for me for a fee. We agreed on two hundred rupees for the whole lot, and thereafter I did not bother with that tedious chore. He charged twenty-five rupees for each set of final proofs. I paid only after the author had okayed the proofs.

The system had worked well until one day he said everything was fine without reading them. I was almost sacked but good sense prevailed after I said that while proofreaders could be hired off the street, where would they find someone to replace me? Having gone through three economics editors in the seven months before I joined, they had decided to keep me on. The following year I landed a bestseller in the economics of marketing and they gave me a handsome bonus.

I told Nikki one day that it was a bad idea for racehorses to pull carts.

'What do you mean?' she asked.

'Well, look at you,' I said, 'you should be a branch manager.'

The branches were where the real clout lay. The four

we had had been around for a hundred and seven years whereas we in editorial were the Johnny-come-latelies. Their main job had been to sell books published in England. In that sense, the book publishing industry had been no different from any of the other industries during the Raj. Britain produced and the colonies bought. Their mainstay was school textbooks.

Then in the mid-1960s, the government decided to end their monopoly. And we had been taken on to develop an alternative college-level list authored by Indians to make up for the loss of revenue caused by the nationalization of school textbooks. But this was always a bit of a pipe-dream.

On our part, we regarded the branches as a bull-pen for ill-educated philistines who saw only the price and thickness but not the value of a book. They, on the other hand, thought we were wet-behind-the-ears-hoity-toity-half-wits from fancy colleges who would bankrupt the company with our airy-fairy ideas. Then there was the old problem of learnt-on-the-job seniority and tradition versus education and iconoclasm.

In all this, the whimsical managing director held the casting vote. But he never took his eyes off the money, to be made or to be saved. It was the *dividet et impera* principle, all very British. After all, it was a British company where we sahibs were still served tea in proper crockery twice a day in the boss's room at eleven and four while the rest had to make do with sipping from chipped mugs on the balcony. After a while, depending on the weather, I started alternating between the two venues. Sometimes Nikki would also come there. But that was rare.

'And you should not have to read proofs, right?'

'Yes, that too,' I had replied.

To her credit, she had agreed and employed a retired copy editor on a part-time basis to take a last lingering look at all final proofs. 'It's cheaper this way,' she had told the managing director.

But the victory had not come cheaply. Nikki had called me in one day and told me that the managing director wanted me to deliver three star writers in economics or management in the next twelve months.

'You fail and you are out, he says.' I had told her to get London off our backs but she had just laughed.

• • •

The meeting started on the dot, all present and awake. It was the last Monday of the month which meant it was not just the week's review but also the month's. We went through all the tedious bits which formed the nuts and bolts of the whole endeavour. No one had anything interesting to report. It was June after all, the slack season for editorial. The suppliers of content for our jobs, the authors, were mostly from teaching establishments and would be away for the summer vacation or finalizing their manuscripts before their establishments opened. One way or another, there wasn't much to do.

This was the time when the editors were sent off for two weeks each to scout for manuscripts. That involved visiting a dozen institutions in whichever region we chose to go. Most of the time was spent on travel because we were allowed only train fare. Mercifully, air conditioning was now available on almost all trains. We did mostly night hops of eight-to-ten hours, washed and changed in the waiting rooms and went off to the colleges we had on our lists. I used to enjoy these travels.

The fellow deputed to attend the weekly reviews from marketing was new, and only a little older than me. He was the sixth since I had joined the firm. I was told they came and went and anyway no one paid much attention to them.

It was, I later discovered, a part of the pretence that we mattered. But it was silly because, as I found, being on good terms with them could be very helpful. They could and did bump up the sales of books on your list, as they had on mine, if you treated them properly.

The truth, whether we acknowledged it or not, was that they were at the sharp end of the business whereas we were quite often only indulging our middle-class pretensions to intellect. As someone had cuttingly said once, all editors in publishing are failed writers, or as in our case, academics. The irony was that having not made it to where the writers and the academics had, we now stood on judgement on their work.

'I have been asked by my boss to tell you all,' the marketing fellow said, 'that of the thirty-two titles published during January-May, twenty have sold around two hundred, ten around four hundred and only two have sold over five hundred and fifty. Of the duds, nearly three-quarters are from the humanities. One of the two that have sold over five hundred copies is from economics; the other is from current affairs. Thank you.'

This was an old story. It wasn't that the books were bad. It was simply that colleges and universities allocated very little money for literature, history, culture and so on. Science got the lion's share at about sixty per cent although the number of students who were enrolled for the courses was a fraction of those enrolled for the humanities where the qualifying marks were lower. The remaining forty-odd per cent was shared by all other disciplines. But even there economics, management and commerce soaked up around a quarter of the money. Of the little that was left for the rest, ninety per cent went on textbooks in the humanities.

The result was poor sales of monographs. Every year, ninety per cent of the remaindered stock comprised titles from the humanities list. In fact, but for Nikhila's insistence, the managing director would have shut down the humanities list long ago.

'They sell well enough abroad,' she had argued more than once. This was true in terms of revenue but not in terms of volumes. 'We need to have a good-looking and complete catalogue, as well.'

The meeting ended with the usual recriminations from Janaki Bose, who handled humanities. She was around fifty-five, tall, thin and angular not just in shape but also in her approach. Quick to take offence and ever ready to say biting things, she let the marketing department have it every month. We had all heard it before, the others more often than I, but no one stopped her. She could be brutal in her put-downs so no one dared, not even Nikhila. In a way, I felt sorry for her because she had come up with some superb titles. This was despite the fact that she had never studied humanities. Her master's was in physics. Once, when we were standing on the balcony, smoking, I had asked her about it.

'I don't know,' she had replied, 'but it may have something to do with my training in precise statements. I hate waffle and I think the readers do, too. Such books do well, perhaps.'

I had felt a little ashamed that even after nearly a year in the firm I had never bothered to give the books on her list even a cursory browse. Later that morning I asked the marketing fellows which of her books had sold the most and to send me a copy. It arrived the next day, a battered looking salesmen's copy. They would not, if they could help it, send one in mint condition. It was by a historian called Arvind Shukla and was about a truly extraordinary range of issues in ancient Indian history. The writing was sharp and the analysis, even though somewhat Marxian in its moorings, was so well arranged that there really was no arguing with it.

I decided to spend more time chatting to Ms Bose, as she encouraged everyone to call her. She didn't seem to mind and introduced me to historiography, the method of history and the notion that large events in history were caused by trivia.

'Like Napoleon would have won at Waterloo if he

hadn't had a runny tum the previous night and started the battle late, allowing Blücher to get there in time?' I asked. 'Or Henry the Eight's priapism?'

'Precisely that,' she had replied. 'Or Gandhi getting thrown off the train at Pietermaritzburg. The Marxists carry on about the so-called 'forces' of history but the truth is that it is just the wisps of fate, if you will, and the twists and turns of fortune. There is neither a grand design nor any inevitability. Things happen, that's all.'

On my way back to my room I stopped by my secretary's table. Mrs Singhal was a retired lady of about sixty from one of the government offices. She had been trained well by the British and Indian burra sahibs and understood the requirements of her job better than the young girls who could not match her for error-free typing and instant-retrieval filing.

I knew she could do with some extra income so I asked her if she would type up a manuscript on her private time. She said yes and a little later, as I left for the day, I gave her Mala Auntie's manuscript. One plus two, I said, as I handed her a hundred rupees as advance. She would need some of that to buy the paper, typing ribbons and carbon sheets. She silently handed me a letter which I folded and put in my pocket and drove back home which I reached as usual by six.

There wasn't much to do, so I went for a walk and thought about Mala Auntie's manuscript. I had spent a couple of hours reading it and was very surprised that she could write so well. There was no reason for me to have thought otherwise, but good writing from unexpected quarters always made me pause.

It was a simple story, about a small town shopkeeper who was coping with the changes that independence had brought. I had had no idea that she could empathize with that class of people or could be so observant or that the change had been so over-arching. I decided to ask her about it when I took the typed manuscript back to her. Then I bought some cigarettes and a record by Mallikarjun Mansur and walked back home where I found Mike and Shiv. Mike was looking furious.

He had just returned from a flight to Kuwait and had brought back a gizmo called VCR, short for video cassette recorder. I had heard of them but had never seen one. It worked like a normal cassette recorder on which we used to hear music but played moving pictures instead recorded on enormous cassettes the size of a demy octavo book. Mike had brought along a couple of films that had been recorded on these things and was anxious to watch them. The two of them had been trying to set the machine up, which just wouldn't come on.

It was Shiv who discovered why. The machine was American and ran on 110 volts whereas in India our machines ran on 220 volts. Mike went berserk and started yelling about Arab cheats. I reminded him that there was no way the salesman could have known Indian voltage, nor even where Mike was going. It didn't help. Mike only got angrier and eventually stomped out leaving Shiv in splits.

'Stupid pilot brain,' he said. 'All he has to do is to get a voltage converter.'

I had no idea such things existed and was astonished that Shiv did. When I asked him about it he said he had bought one in Oxford for his American six-piece toaster, of all things. He said he had bought it there and made the same mistake as Mike.

He went off to tell Mike and see if they could buy one somewhere. They both came back after a couple of hours with the converter in Shiv's ever-present cloth bag. They plugged all the things in and the VCR came on. We spent the rest of the evening watching *Godfather* till well past one in the morning on my black and white EC TV. It had come with the flat, dumped there by the landlord when he got himself a new one.

• • •

It was only after dinner as I was lighting a cigarette that I remembered the letter Mrs Singhal had given me. I fetched it from the bedroom and read it. It wasn't addressed to me by name but to the economics editor and it offered a manuscript for publication. The writer was one Madhavi Raghuraman. She said she had just completed her PhD at Rochester in the US. The topic was 'Aggregating Political Preferences of the Constituents of a Federation.'

'I have tried,' she wrote, 'to apply some well-known tools of economic analysis to political science. I have obtained the intriguing result that India runs a real risk of making Selig Harrison's dire prophecies about the Balkanization of India come true because, mathematically at least, the problem has no solution, or more precisely, the solution is so feeble and constrained that it is as good as a no-solution.'

She said further that she would be in India during July and August and would like to call on the editors.

After four years in publishing I had acquired a horrible habit. The first thought to cross my mind was 'five hundred copies'. The second was 'three hundred and fifty rupees' which was a premium price. The third was 'who could referee it?'

It was going to be a very tiresome battle with the marketing department but I knew eventually I would win. The referee problem was more difficult. From the few lines in Ms Raghuraman's letter it was clear that it would have to be sent abroad. The foreign academics demanded a lot more money than we could pay. That meant we had to get London's help and that led to its own problems, the worst of which was their demanding and getting the author for their own list. In the end, I decided to ask one of my professors and see if he would make the effort for double the usual fee of three hundred rupees. I felt sure Nikhila would agree when I explained why.

Later, I wondered whether I had decided to publish it even before taking a look at it because I liked the way the letter was written or whether because the topic was so relevant. It had happened to me a few times before, when some gut feel or instinct had prompted me to push hard for a title. That, in fact, was how I had won the five-hundred copy print-run battle with marketing. Such manuscripts needed to be in the libraries as a book, and not as a mere entry in the list of doctoral theses submitted and accepted but inaccessible to future researchers.

3

The monsoon eventually came. The rain began slowly at first, just a shower now and then. But in mid-July on just the night I had to go to the airport to fetch some people, it burst forth in its fullest majesty. The car stalled on the way to the airport, one of a few hundred others. I waded through waist-deep water, losing my shoes in the mud, slipping into a deep hole and soaked to the skin. Eventually, after about two hours they came out of the customs area.

It took another forty minutes to get a taxi and by the time I returned home after dropping them off, dawn was breaking. I showered, drank some coffee, read the paper and waited for the man who came to clean the car and the lady who came to cook and clean. He showed up at seven as usual. I gave him some money and asked to get the car fixed by the time I came back from office. He said all right and, as usual, was as good as his word.

But the cooking lady didn't turn up. Instead, she sent her young daughters, who were on their way to school, to tell me that she wouldn't be coming in that day. This happened from time to time when her husband got drunk and passed out. She needed to be home when he woke up, she had told me once.

Sunidhi had disapproved, sometimes quite forcefully, of my reliance on servants. She even insisted that I travel by bus. Once when we were out for dinner at someone's house she had made several snide remarks about my being a laat saab. I told her off in no uncertain terms when I dropped her off later that evening. She refused to see me for two weeks after that. It should have been clear to me that it wasn't a match made in heaven but you know how it is with these things.

It was important that I have the car that evening because I had promised some friends to go for a concert at Kamani Auditorium on Lytton Road. They had moved from Bombay recently and were waiting for their car to arrive. The Indian Railways had been doing its best but what with this and that, the official at the enquiry counter said, you could never tell when exactly a goods train would show up.

'Keep checking every day,' he told my friend's husband Ashok. 'The demurrage is quite high.'

Like all concerts in India, this one also started at an awkward time. Seven in the evening is too early for dinner. And it finished at ten thirty, which is too late for it. In-between, concert-goers have the choice of eating oily junk food at exorbitant prices that the organizers sold in the foyer. But Ashok's wife Sharada who was a veteran concert-goer had beaten the system. In return for the lift, she had packed dinner in a large tiffin-carrier which she placed on the seat beside her at the back.

'We can drive down to India Gate during the break,' she said. Ashok looked embarrassed but saw the point. So other than muttering something about looking silly, he kept quiet.

The concert turned out to be quite sub-standard. First, the prima donna came late and then said she had a bad throat. She sang for less than an hour before lapsing into a sullen silence and let her junior stand in for her. Tired after a full day at work and no sleep the previous night, I dozed off. By eight-thirty, Sharada was ready to go. We drove to the stretch of lawn behind Vigyan Bhavan. The grass was very wet so we kept the food on the bonnet and ate standing up. It had been very long since I had eaten genuine home-cooked Tamil food. I ate in silence and listened to Ashok and Sharada chatting amicably about nothing in particular. They seemed well-matched and I wondered who had made the bigger effort to get the gears to mesh properly.

Sharada and I had been in school together for a couple of years. Her parents lived a few houses away and being fellow-Tamils, were frequent visitors to our house. She was a Plain Jane but made up for it with her brains. We used to study together before the exams. But for her, I doubt if I would have passed.

Her mother used to make her part her hair in the middle and put a maroon bindi two inches below the parting in what appeared to me to be a horizontal exclamation mark.

I used to tease her about it, asking why either the bindi or the parting could not be to one side or on opposite sides or why there could not be two of each. She promised to find out but never did. I have asked the same question to dozens of women since then with the same result. Most of them have told me not to be so silly.

Over the years we had kept in intermittent touch and when she had moved to Delhi with her husband three months ago, she had phoned me. Ashok, she said, was head-hunted for her a few years ago and they'd got married. They didn't have any children, not yet anyway. I barely knew him but aside from being slightly wary of his very Brahmin attitudes, I got on well enough with him.

He had a simple approach to other people: their habits and behaviour, even if deplorable, were their business. Sharada told me it came from having been brought up in a very insular Tamil Brahmin family from somewhere deep in the south.

'Their house is in the temple agraharam. You must curb your natural tendency for silliness.'

He was a banker and had a degree in economics from Manchester. He read a lot and had introduced me to two very fine and very English writers, Anthony Burgess and Iris Murdoch. Burgess handled the language like Gibbsy used to handle his Java, with a deftness that made all your senses tingle. Murdoch was lugubrious but in a deeply tasteful way. The two could not have been more different in their backgrounds but both managed to produce sublime writing.

'I hear a cousin of mine is coming to visit you.'

Sharada said, when we were driving back to their home. I asked her who that might be and she said Madhavi Raghuraman.

'She is going to stay with us for a month before she returns to the US. Bright girl but in a very insistent sort of way,' she added. It was an odd sort of adjective to use but a couple of weeks later I saw what she meant.

• • •

On a Sunday evening a couple of weeks later I was sitting dejectedly on the verandah watching the rain, thinking about Sunidhi. I had a rule that I would not have my first drink till seven-thirty. There was still half an hour to go when the phone rang. I let it ring on till the caller hung up. But sometime later it rang again and this time, since I was near the phone, I answered it. It was Sharada.

'Can you meet my cousin tomorrow?' she asked.

I asked if eleven-thirty in the office would be all right and, after a shouted question to her cousin, she said it would.

'Fine,' I replied and rang off wondering what the cousin would be like.

The next morning, just after the morning tea ceremony, Mrs Singhal, who belonged to the generation of Indian women who insisted that all women should cover themselves as much as they could, provided it was not by a burqa, buzzed me on the intercom.

'There's someone to see you, Sir,' she said. I had got to know her well enough to detect the tones in her voice.

The only time she had sounded more disapproving was when a long-haired economist from Tulsa, Oklahoma, had come to see me about a manuscript. Unless you were a Sikh, she believed, men should have short hair.

Ms Madhavi Raghuraman, Rochester, NY, was about my age, dressed in beige baggy shorts that stopped an acceptable inch short of her knees, a floppy black T-shirt, tan sandals, goggles, and hair that fell to her shoulders. She had the classic South Asian features, tallish, maybe five-seven, slender in a well-built sort of way. But it was her eyes that defined her: large, brown and lively. I stood up and shook hands which were surprisingly rough. I asked her to sit down and buzzed Mrs Singhal for some tea. She told me her mother and Sharada's were sisters.

'I used to hear a lot about you from Sharada till about fifteen years ago,' she said. 'Then you vanished.'

'Well, her father was posted out. I suppose that's why.'

'Sharada told me about how you pestered her about the bindis and the parting.'

'And do you know why they are arranged the way they are? Or why there aren't two of each?'

'It's to do with the idea that symmetry is nicer to look at than asymmetry,' she said. 'I have no idea why that should be so but if you look carefully you will find that the two eyes and ears and the single nose balance the bindi and the parting perfectly.'

'In that case, you can just as well have a horizontal

parting and five bindis, you know two on either side and one in the centre.'

'The bindi also serves to highlight the forehead. The subtler the bindi the nicer it looks. Some silly women wear these huge bindis. That defeats the entire purpose of the bindi.'

The tea came. I poured it for her. She asked for two spoons of sugar and lots of milk. I asked her what we could do for her.

She pulled out some typed pages from her bag and handed them over to me. 'This is the summary of what I have done, my PhD thesis. Can you publish it?'

I asked her to leave it with me and that I would get back within a few days. We talked a bit more about this and that. She got up to leave and then I did something I only did for some of our really big authors. I walked her down four flights of stairs to where her car, a grey Fiat, was parked.

'Sharada was wondering if you were free to come for lunch this Saturday,' she said as I opened the door for her. I said I would and she drove off, leaving me with a mild sense of longing. I smoked a cigarette and trudged back up the four flights.

• • •

To my slight surprise, I found the days dragging. Usually, the week went by quickly and it was the weekends that dragged. I read the synopsis that Madhavi had left with me. At one level, like most of economics, it was making an obvious point about how hard it is to convert several different preferences into a single big preference that satisfied everyone. But so far the argument had been made only for individuals, not states in a federation. She was extending it to collectives and that, I thought, was quite clever of her.

I feared that there would be a lot of abstruse mathematics in the text which would dissuade the marketing fellows who'd say it would sell a hundred copies only. So I foresaw a battle ahead. But all that was well into the future. First the manuscript had to get the referee's approval and that could by no means be taken for granted. I decided not to take any chances and to send it to Arun Ganguly who taught this sort of thing at the university. He could be annoyingly pedantic but at least he would understand what it was all about.

I had a few errands to run on Saturday and it was nearly one-thirty by the time I reached Sharada's flat. It was in one of those government complexes that scar the face of South Delhi. My father too had worked for the government but he had lived in bungalows with at least an acre of lawn and garden. We had never lived in a flat.

But a lot of my friends work for the government and live in the new but cramped 'quarters' as they are called. I have often wondered how the government could commandeer the best land, build absolutely the worst flats and put the brightest people that India had to offer in them. It was almost as if the quality of the housing and its location were inversely proportional.

Central Delhi had been built by an English

fellow called Lutyens, pronounced as Luiyens and not Loot-yenj, for the ICS officers. It was like living in a manicured forest. When we had lived there in the late 1950s and early 1960s, it was the only Delhi there was, apart from Old Delhi and the beyond-the-pale areas where the refugees from Pakistan lived, like Rajinder Nagar to the west and Jangpura to the south. Delhi was defined by the Yamuna on one side and the Inner Ring Road elsewhere. The atmosphere, the bucolic ambience and the prevailing colonial culture have gone forever now.

I knew every back lane and alley in the area. They were very dimly lit and my friends and I have seen some very romantic goings-on there, mostly the servant crowd but also, once in a while, the sons and daughters of the sahibs. Once, driving past Nehru's house, while dropping a friend to the airport, my father forgot I was sitting on the back seat. He pointed to the little cottage there and said that was where Padmaja Naidu had lived. The two of them giggled for a long time. It was only much later that I found out what had been so funny.

In 1972, three youngsters drove into Indira Gandhi's residence, hooped a few times, and drove out. The single policeman outside had looked on indulgently but Mrs Gandhi had taken one of my uncles, who was the police chief, to task. 'They actually blew their horn,' she had told him indignantly. He had left instructions that the gate was not to be kept open. But no more policemen had been put on sentry duty outside her house. The

Gymkhana Club, which was opposite her house, was the social hub with its own Empire Stores and petrol pump manned by a very fat man called Bholu. My mother did a lot of her shopping there.

Now, the once spiffy bungalows have become quite dilapidated. They had always been very uncomfortable to live in anyway. We used to spend most of our time on the verandahs. Except at the height of winter, we even slept there. Desert coolers were just coming into the market and air conditioners were very rare. Recently, I had told a visiting Brit that, growing up, I had never really slept in a bedroom. He had been completely taken aback. It was only later that I realized how extraordinary that must have sounded to him.

• • •

I was the last to arrive. Sharada had called two other couples from Ashok's office. Madhavi was wearing a maroon cotton sari. I had noticed how Indian women regard an event as being formal or informal depending on who they are meeting, and not for what. So Madhavi, in spite of her years in the US, had turned up for a formal meeting at her publisher's in shorts and T-shirt but was dressed for an informal Saturday lunch at her cousin's home in a sari. She looked taller and more graceful than she had done on Monday.

'Well, hello,' she said, 'welcome.'

'Hi, how are you? Sorry I am late.'

'That's okay. What will you have to drink? We only have some beer and vodka.'

I settled down with a super-chilled beer and was introduced to the others. All four were bankers and Ashok's colleagues. So after a while they lost interest in me, preferring instead to carry office talk home which was mostly about postings and transfers and the usual petty jealousies that are the hallmark of such talk. I got up and strolled out to the balcony for a smoke where Sharada joined me.

'Bored?' she asked.

'Not at all, I just needed to smoke.'

We chatted for a few minutes and presently she went off to make sure everything was all right in the kitchen.

'The chicken,' she said as she went. 'I have to see if it has come out all right.'

I decided to smoke another cigarette and was halfway through it when Madhavi came out to tell me that lunch was served.

'Let me get you another beer,' she said.

The dining table could seat only six but Sharada said that was fine as she and Madhavi would pull up chairs at the corners. She sat in the corner between me and Ashok and Madhavi sat between the two men at the opposite corner. Lunch wore on. The food was exquisite. We got done finally at about three. The beer, the heavy food and the hot humid weather had made everyone sleepy and after a few awkward moments, I stood up to leave. The other couples quickly stood up, too. Ashok and Sharada came down to see off the office colleagues. Madhavi also came down.

'Sorry about that,' she said as I sat at the wheel and

rolled down the window. 'The other couples were an afterthought added on by Sharada who said it would serve as a return lunch for them.'

'That's okay,' I said. 'The food was terrific.'

'It was, wasn't it? Sharada is a great cook when she puts her mind to it.'

I asked her if she was free that evening and if so, would she like to come for a drive around Delhi. She said all right and I arranged to pick her up at about seven from the market down the road.

'Sharada will start match-making otherwise,' she said grimly as I let in the clutch. 'She could challenge Gale and Shapely anytime,' she added cryptically.

I reached home, had a quick shower and went straight to bed. By the time I woke up it was almost six-thirty and after another shower and a quick drink straight from the bottle, I drove back to the market near Sharada's house. I was just in time to see Madhavi walking down the road. She was dressed this time in a white salwar and red kurta and smelt of Cuticura talcum powder.

'I will have to be back by eight thirty,' she said as she got in. 'Dinner is at eight forty-five or so.' I drove to India Gate and we ate some ice cream or actually rather a lot of it. I asked her who Gale and Shapely were and she told me they were two mathematicians-turned-economists who had tried to solve the problem of stable pairings.

'It's called the stable marriage problem but that is just a convenience. It is used in a variety of more important applications.'

I got a short lecture on how roommates in hostels and medical residents in hospitals posed special problems of pairing and how the Gale-Shapley theorem helped pair them in a stable way. Economists, I thought, could worm their way into any problem.

I told her a bit about myself. There wasn't much to tell. After my master's I had tried my hand at research but had given it up in favour of law which I also gave up after I was eighty per cent through the course. Three years after my MA I had found a job which satisfied all my needs—academic, status, money and free time.

'Now I am content,' I told her. 'Perfect equilibrium in, your language. No desire to move.'

She asked me a lot more questions than I had asked her and came dangerously close once to asking about girlfriends. I changed the subject by taking it back to Gale and Shapely and was amused to see how animated she became the moment she got the chance to talk on that sort of thing.

Her father, she told me on the way back, had been in the railways. It had been an itinerant life, not unlike mine. I had attended five schools in eleven years, she six. I had been instructed in three languages, she in four. We took bets on who was the more confused and agreed to find out before she went back to the US.

I dropped her back and since it was still quite early, I decided to see if Mike was home. Mala Auntie said he was in bed with a slight fever. I went up to his room and found him propped up with an Asterix comic. That was the only reading he would buy when he flew to some Western destination.

'Can't take anything more,' he said when I asked him to read something else. 'By the way, do you want to go to England? I have a free ticket for Mummy but she says she can't come now and Daddy won't travel without her.'

'Can I travel when you are flying the plane?' I asked.

'Yes, of course, provided you can get a seat at short notice. This is a subject-to-load ticket which means you get on at the last minute after all chances of selling another ticket have disappeared.'

I said okay. It would be free and fun with Mike around. And if it happened in August there would also be free board and lodging at Debbie's place. I then went down to get a drink and found the Brigadier rummaging about in the fridge.

'No ice,' he said.

He handed me a bottle of whiskey and a bottle of cold water. I went back up and gave Mike a small one. He gulped it down and asked for another. After an hour or so I went home.

• • •

On Monday morning Mrs Singhal handed me the typed copy of Mala Auntie's manuscript. I paid her the rest of the money and after she had left, I opened the package. It had been put neatly in a file for easy reading and I settled down for a quick glance through it. All the others had gone off to the hills for the week and I was holding the fort. My job was to send signed routine acknowledgements to incoming mail and say a detailed response would follow shortly. This involved signing around thirty letters, that's all.

By lunchtime I had finished reading Mala Auntie's manuscript. It wasn't up our street as we didn't do fiction. Nevertheless I thought I'd show it to Nikhila who could decide. By three, I had signed the letters and there wasn't really anything further. So I put one copy in my bag and left for the day. When I got home I found the Jolly Roger was up. I turned around and left and, without quite realizing it, found myself at Sharada's doorstep. Like the fellow in the Belafonte calypso who was attracted to the church by the smell of food, I too had come unbidden. For a moment I wondered if I should ring the bell or quietly go away. After a few moments, I pressed the doorbell.

Sharada opened the door, a mug of coffee in her hand. She didn't seem at all surprised. She didn't quite say that she was expecting me but she didn't have to. She led the way silently to the dining table where she poured me a cup of coffee. Madhavi, dressed this time in a kaftan, was drinking tea. She pushed a plate of biscuits towards me. No one said anything, not even hello.

I asked them if anything was wrong. Sharada said that someone had sent a complaint against Ashok alleging that he had demanded a bribe to sanction a loan.

'He came home after lunch, quite shattered and is sleeping now.'

I asked her if they knew who it was and she said

yes, it was a minor politician from the ruling party. He had demanded a loan without any collateral. Ashok had refused. All this had happened some months ago and Ashok had forgotten all about it till this morning.

'When he reached the office,' said Sharada, 'his general manager called him in and showed him the letter. Ashok had no idea at first what it was about but then he remembered. He told the GM what had happened. The GM told him not to worry and that he would sort it out with the head office because these allegations were common. But Ashok is most distraught. He says this is just the sort of thing that destroys reputations and careers. The whispers will always be there.'

I didn't know what to say and sat silently recalling how some malicious trucker had done something similar to one of my uncles. It had taken three years for the enquiry to be completed and he lost two promotions as a result. His chances of making it to the top were ruined for good. Ashok must have been worried about that as well because until now he was doing better than his competitors and this would be the proverbial invisible spot on his unblemished record. He was only thirty-five and had a long way to go.

A little later, just as I finished my coffee Ashok came out and I thought it would be best to leave. Madhavi came down to see me off.

'Call me about the proposal,' she said 'when you have decided what to do with it. I have met a couple of other publishers as well.'

I told her I needed the manuscript now and would have to get it refereed which was standard procedure. She said she would bring it around later that week and went back up. It was nearly six now and I went home. The Jolly Roger had been put back in its rightful place. The flat was redolent of some rich perfume. It had to be Mike, I thought. Shiv's salary didn't run to imported perfumes.

Mike had left a note. 'Not what you think. I was playing agony aunt.' I briefly wondered who was in such agony that the Jolly Roger had had to be posted for her. Still, if it was privacy they needed, they'd had plenty of it. I phoned Mala Auntie and told her I would bring her manuscript around in the morning. She said she would pack me some eggy breakfast and disconnected.

The evening stretched pointlessly ahead. I sat down to read Mala Auntie's manuscript more thoroughly. It was ten by the time I got up. She had written a tidy little novel of about two hundred and fifty pages. The India of the late 1940s and early 1950s was described not in the usual terms of tube-wells and fertilizer, or steel and electricity, but in terms of ordinary Indians having to deal with other Indians as rulers.

The basic storyline was that in 1948 a small Hindu businessman comes across from Pakistan with only some cash and jewellery. When he tries to start a business everyone helps him in whatever way they can, except the government whose minions start inventing rules to extort bribes from him. After trying to overcome these obstacles for seven years he starts wondering if he should go back to Pakistan. Cleverly, Mala Auntie had ended the story there.

I thought that even that far back it had become clear that ordinary citizens stood no chance whatsoever in free India. Oppression at the macro scale had been replaced by oppression at the micro scale. The British had made up for their political inequities by being extremely fair in administrative terms. In free India, it had become the other way round. So obsessed was the political leadership with their freedoms that it completely forgot that the citizen cared not about large ideas but the small things that had made life bearable under the British.

• • •

It was noon by the time I reached the office the next day. I had started out a few minutes earlier than usual to hand over the typescript to Mala Auntie and found her looking worried. She said the Brigadier was unwell and had not slept the whole night, complaining of some pain in the chest. The driver had reported sick and Mike, who was away on the short flight to Dubai and back, would be home only by eleven.

I offered to drive them to the military hospital which wasn't very far. We packed the Brigadier into the car. He seemed quite alright now and kept protesting, but inwardly I think he was quite relieved that I had arrived.

'Mala worries too much,' he whispered to me.

The army doctors ran some quick checks and said

everything was fine for the moment. Indigestion, they said.

'But better be careful, Sir,' the colonel told him.

They asked him to get a few tests done. I drove them back home and then left with my breakfast for the office.

I found Madhavi waiting for me.

'She has been here since ten,' Mrs Singhal told me. She sounded irritated. Unannounced visits were a strict no-no in her government conditioned book.

'I have been trying your number all morning,' Madhavi said, 'but there was no reply. Where were you?'

'I left early,' I said and told her where I had been. 'What seems to be the problem? Why this unexpected visit? '

She didn't respond for so long that I repeated the question. 'What's the matter?'

'Look, I don't know how to say it but I think there might be a problem with my stupid thesis.'

I waited for her to go on, and after another longish silence she said her supervisor had published a paper in a technical journal and had borrowed heavily from her ideas.

'Luckily, they were not the central theorems so I am all right there. But it is a nuisance to have to spend another six months redoing the thing. My funding runs out in December. I will have to support myself for three months there till March. It's quite expensive.'

I didn't know how to respond. I knew this sort of thing went on. Bright students were particularly at risk. One of my classmates who had gone to a premier American university straight after BA almost went out of his mind when it had happened to him. He had come back to India and spent two more years writing a fresh thesis. What would have taken five years had taken seven.

'It's not actually plagiarism,' she said angrily. 'It's plain theft. Now I will have to rewrite two entire chapters.' I wanted to tell her plagiarism *was* theft but didn't.

A few months earlier, on one of my rounds of the university to scout for manuscripts, I had asked a couple of professors about it. One of them taught economics and the other philosophy. The one who taught philosophy said it was because the economists had unleashed their foolish theories on academia also.

'In this case,' he said, 'it is the one that says competition serves citizens best.'

'They forgot the moral dimensions of competition,' he said. 'Darwinianism may yield the best results in some ways but not in all ways. It tends to debase.'

The economist had responded by saying that offering the best to the citizen was in itself moral while not offering it was immoral. They wrangled on and I listened in fascinated silence, secretly regretting that I had not become a part of this world where even theft was discussed in such a different way.

I tended to agree with the philosophy professor, however. At least where academics were concerned, the need to prove your worth by constantly publishing trivial theorems in journals had blurred the distinction between the truly excellent and the only slightly mediocre. Perhaps my views were biased because the booming journals business was reducing the flow of good manuscripts. Why write a hundred thousand words when five thousand fetched better returns?

Mrs Singhal brought some tea and I unpacked the omelettes and parathas. I was very hungry. There was enough for three people. We ate in silence for a few minutes. She also appeared not to have eaten anything in the morning and was literally wolfing them down.

'So I do nothing with your proposal now, right?' I asked eventually. She nodded, unable to speak through a full mouth.

'Well, yes, but that's not the problem. I want to make a confession. I had sent it to two other publishers and one of them has sent an acceptance letter. I am sorry. I should have told you earlier.'

'That's okay,' I said. 'Write back to them saying "not now dear, I have a headache". Tell them you have to work some more on it. You are under no obligation until the formal contract is signed and even then you are not under any compulsion to deliver. I have a dozen such would-be authors on my list.'

'Yes, that's what Ashok also said this morning. But sorry nevertheless. I ought to have told you much earlier.'

After she had gone it occurred to me that she need not have come all the way to tell me this. She could easily have phoned later in the day or in the evening after I got home. I felt a sudden thrill of pleasure, of the sort I had not felt for months. I went out to the balcony and smoked two cigarettes.

• • •

I left office early because I wanted to be at the Flying Club in Safdarjung by four. I had become member of the Gliding Club soon after Sunidhi had gone off. That was the only time I felt relieved about her departure because she had prevented me from joining for eighteen whole months.

'Elitist,' she had said. 'Insensitive. I won't allow it.'

Yes, allow. I had wagged my tail obediently. Being a very rich girl herself she felt doubly for the poor. She would start crying when she saw little children begging on the road.

The afternoon is hardly a good time to be driving a bike on the roads of Delhi. The heat and humidity can be awful. The ever-present dust makes it worse and the Flying Club would be closed if visibility was poor. But there had been a storm the previous evening, one of those typical Delhi things that start just when the offices close and end when you reach home.

This one had blown hard for a couple of hours, as against the summer storm norm of about thirty minutes. The result was a clear blue sky, which meant the atmospheric pressure was high and a good day to try gliding. There was a light breeze as well, as the wind sock showed and the thermometer in the club office said the temperature was around 35 degrees centigrade. Ideal conditions for gliding.

I helped the attendant push the glider out and the instructor asked me to get off quickly. I went through the usual drill and then, on a signal from the instructor, the winch started pulling, slowly at first and then faster. When we reached the required speed I pulled the stick back and climbed over the Pakistan embassy, turned left towards Moti Bagh, flew on to the RK Puram multi-storey flats, turned left on Ring Road, flew till AIIMs, turned left, and landed across the Safdarjung flyover, taking care to keep the tail well away from its parapet. If you brushed it, you could break many bones, if not the neck or the spine. Five minutes from start to finish.

The basic circuit done, I asked for permission to go up again and glide for fifteen minutes. There was no one else queuing up for his turn and the instructor agreed. But as usual he told me to stay close to the airport. I went back up, found a cheel in a thermal over Ashok Hotel, flew into it, and floated around in tight circles over Gymkhana Club and Vigyan Bhavan. The loud hiss of the air, the occasional sound of a horn from below, trees as far as I could see, made the flight at four in the afternoon worth it.

The smoothness with which the glider leaves the ground gives the watcher no indication at all of the strength required to pull the stick back for getting the machine off the ground. Nor of the juddering that starts on the rudder pedals at your feet as soon as you get airborne. It takes all your strength to climb and stay up. You can't see the air but it is exactly like the sea, resistant and rolling. You need a lot of strength and stamina.

There is an added risk in a glider. It's very easy for it to fall out of the sky because it has no power. It's like going downhill in a car whose engine has stopped and whose brakes are iffy. In a glider if your speed drops below the critical minimum you can go down like a stone. That and the new environment of being in the air, rather than on terra firma, ensure that it's only after a dozen or so times that you learn the knack flying and can pay attention to things around and below you.

How to avoid stalling is the second thing the instructor taught me the very first time we went up. And he did it very dramatically so that I would never forget. He told me to climb, and like a fool I pulled the stick back forgetting that there was no engine. Within ten seconds the glider was falling to the ground and I thought I was done for. It was mind-numbing fear, of the sort I had never ever felt before.

Then after falling for about 300 feet from the 900 we were at, he put the thing into a steep dive. Since I was sitting in the front I could see the ground near Kidwai Nagar rushing up towards us and I almost peed in my pants with terror. About thirty seconds later, when the speed had got back up to around 50mph, he did something with the controls and the glider levelled out. Another half a minute or so later we landed. I was shivering with fear, my knees were wobbly and when I climbed out, my legs just folded up. The instructor laughed, gave me a friendly kick with an accompanying abuse and walked away. Darega to marega nahin, he said, echoing the saying that there are bold pilots and there are old pilots, but there are no old and bold pilots.

He was around fifty and very taciturn. He had been in the Indian Air Force before retirement a few years ago and had found this job at the Flying Club. From Canberras to gliders wasn't a good exchange but the air force had so few planes that they retired their pilots when they turned forty-five.

It was only after fifty or so takeoffs and landings that the instructor had allowed me to go solo. On my fifteenth solo, he didn't bother to come out of his office when my turn came. I had learnt the ropes. I had been flying solo since then, exulting each time I went up at how annoyed Sunidhi would have been at this brazen extravagance.

It was past seven by the time I got home. I was very hungry and wondered whether I should eat something now or wait for dinner to be served at eight-thirty, as it were, because that was when the lady who cooked had to go off. If I wanted to eat later, which I usually did because I wasn't done with the drinking by then, I would have to get the food out myself. But that was a bore. And if I ate now I wouldn't be hungry enough at eight-thirty. When I told Sunidhi about this dilemma she had said I should get myself something called a hot case and, in fact, I had got one. But I didn't fancy eating out of those things and had given it to the man who cleaned the car soon after Sunidhi had left. It was one less thing that reminded me of her.

I showered, changed and poured myself a huge drink even by my standards, a sign of creeping contentment after a long time. But since I had to eat something I decided to walk down to the market which was just 500 yards away to get a bun-omelette, my staple snack. The barrow boy who sold the bun-omelettes had tuned his transistor radio to the news instead of the usual Vividh Bharati channel, the only entertainment wavelength that was permitted.

The home minister, said the newsreader, had assured the country that the government wasn't about to fall. The barrow boy laughed and said Indira Gandhi would soon come back to power. I had no interest in politics, which was another irritant for Sunidhi. Hedonist, she had called me. I had to look it up in her OED.

I paid for my bun-omelette and returned home to drink and think about Ms Raghuraman while I waited for dinner.

4

It's always been something of a mystery to me as to why doctors' waiting rooms have old and very old magazines strewn about on a centre table. Can the sick actually read? That too in a doctor's antechamber? I had never seen anyone doing so but it wasn't very often that I visited doctors. The last time had been five years ago when a friendly doctor had suggested I might have leprosy and had ordered a skin biopsy. It had taken a very fraught month for the results to come out.

'It's a very English affectation,' said the Brigadier when I mentioned the magazines to him. 'It helps them avoid each other's eyes.'

We were awaiting our turn in the military hospital. Mala Auntie had phoned a few days ago to ask if I would take the Brigadier for his check-up. 'Mukhbir,' she said, 'is on a flight but he will join you both at the hospital.'

I hadn't heard from Madhavi after that day and as usual was at a loose end over the weekend. So I had driven over and picked the Brigadier up. We had arrived at the hospital in good time only to find that there were about fifteen others waiting before us. The

Brigadier was inclined to call off the whole thing but I persuaded him to stay. I was scared of irritating Mala Auntie. Anyway, I had been entrusted with a job and it had to be done.

We had been waiting for over an hour when the nurse finally asked the Brigadier, who had dozed off, to go in. Mike walked in a few minutes later, saw me and came over. We sat quietly till the Brigadier came out with a broad smile on his face. He said the doctor had given the usual warnings about eating and drinking less but was happy overall.

Mike and I went out to the parking lot while he got his next appointment. It was almost one o'clock by the time we drove out of the hospital complex which, despite its manicured lawns and huge old trees, was not a very cheerful place.

'Since now I have been told officially that I am perfectly all right, I think I will have a beer and some butter chicken,' the Brigadier said. He told Mike who was driving to go to the club.

'Gym or Defence?' asked Mike.

I said they could come to mine. 'I have just become a member and have been meaning to take you all there.'

I should have asked if we should pick Mala Auntie up. But the Brigadier was looking so happy that I decided not to. It wasn't that she would not allow him to eat and drink whatever he wanted; it was just that she would limit the quantities to virtually nothing. Neither of them said anything either, except Mike who said he would call her from the club and tell her we would not be home for lunch.

'She will be annoyed,' he said, 'but I am sure Daddy's good news will help.'

My club was a modern affair, set adjacent to the Lodhi Gardens. It looked like a good three-star hotel. The air conditioning was fierce, the carpeting soft, the furniture uncomfortable and the waiters smart. The contrast with the standard-issue British club, with its freshly painted shabbiness and pervasive air of mourning accentuated by doddering waiters, was stark. I had to reassure the Brigadier that this was indeed a club and not a hotel. 'They don't like to call it a club,' I told him. 'It is called an "International Centre".'

I had once asked a designer friend of mine about the comfort in the old clubs and its absence in the new ones. 'The key difference between an old Brit-style colonial club and a modern Indian was one of purpose. For them the club was a refuge where they wanted to spend long hours comfortably; for us it is just a place where we go to eat and show off that we are members.'

'But why are the chairs and sofas so uncomfortable in ours and not in theirs?'

'It's to do with the length and width of the seats on them. The seat should be at least twenty inches from back to front but that costs more. So we make do with awkward lengths that give no support at all to the thighs. We also put in straight-backed dining chairs because they cost less. Even a slight incline to the backrest costs more.'

The cold beer settled the Brigadier's doubts about my club. The starters, when they arrived, were served properly. The Brigadier perked up and told us about his first time in a club.

'My first posting was at Miranshaw in 1945,' he said. 'Only a dozen or so old useless Brits had been left there. There wasn't much left to do. We were at the fag end of the war. I was nearly thirty years younger than the youngest of them, a flatulent major called Birkenshaw who had been sent off from Burma to cool his heels.

'The Brits kept to themselves and ignored the Indians. The ritual required me to introduce myself to them. I went around telling them my name and rank and, you know, there wasn't even a grunt of acknowledgement from any of them. I could have been one of the waiters. Mind, I had been to Sandhurst, which none of them had. Fools.'

The anger had subsided to mere indignation after all these years but the hurt was still there. We ended up having three bottles of beer each. Then the Brigadier ordered a whole of lot of meat, chicken, fish and rice. I got the leftovers packed and we argued over whether they should take them for Mala Auntie or whether I should take them home for dinner. They won. It wouldn't do at all, said father and son, for Mala Auntie to know what the Brigadier had eaten.

It was three-thirty by the time we left and this time I drove because Mike, after his long flight, was falling asleep. I dropped them off and went home hoping that the Jolly Roger would not be up. It wasn't and I quickly fell asleep.

The phone woke me. Madhavi was on the line.

It was nearly seven. 'Can you come for dinner?' she asked. 'I am leaving in three days so Sharada decided to call some people. Can you come a little early, say by seven-thirty?'

I wasn't feeling particularly up to it but decided to go anyway. By the time I turned up many others had also arrived. We spent a pleasant evening talking, drinking and eating. I caught Madhavi's eye several times but barely managed to speak to her. As I was leaving she told me she would be in touch.

I went home, inexplicably disconsolate.

• • •

'Well, how goes it with the Moby Dicks?'

Nikki and I were standing on the balcony. A month had passed since Madhavi had gone back to the US. There had been no letter from her. I wondered from time to time about her but for two weeks now the pressure to deliver star authors had increased. This was the second time in as many weeks Nikki was raising the topic.

'I have made a shortlist of nine,' I said. 'I wrote to them last week. Let's see how many respond.'

'I suggest you wait for two weeks and then go over and see them.'

'Six of them don't live here.'

'Never mind. That's all right. Go to them.'

I said I would and on the way in I told her it would take around three weeks to visit the four cities where they lived.

'That's fine,' she said. 'Just get on with it. The boss wants it, so stop raising objections and just do it.'

I didn't mind the travelling as much as the long periods of boredom in the trains and hotels. I had started copying Somerset Maugham who used to carry a sack of books with him whenever he travelled. I made do with a very old and large suitcase that had once belonged to a grand-uncle. He had discarded it after his last visit to my parents' home. It also carried my bedding of three pillows and two sheets.

Sunidhi used to insist that I should carry at least three serious works instead of just a lot of fiction. 'Just count the number of hours when you are doing nothing on the trains and in the hotels. You can spend at least some of that time reading something worthwhile instead of the trash you take with you,' she would say.

Not all of it was but who was to argue. Some of the best writers in England—Kingsley Amis, Anthony Burgess, Martin Amis, J.P. Donleavy, Somerset Maugham, John le Carré, etc., were not trash by any yardstick. But it was simpler to just take along some Levi Strauss, Simone de Beauvoir and that pretentious fellow, Jean-Paul Sartre. I would leave these at the bottom of the suitcase until the return journey, when I would do a quick read through to be prepared for her quizzing. Nothing annoyed her more than my coming back without having at least opened them. After a couple of long sulks I had started taking precautions. She meant well but could be a bit too earnest sometimes.

Now that travel had become imminent and sacking

had become a distinct possibility, I turned my full attention to undertaking the one to prevent the other. My first priority was to collect around twenty-five books for the three-week trip. I had been caught short once on a dog-leg through Orissa and Madhya Pradesh and spent a miserable nine bookless days. I had sworn never to let it happen again. So I told Nikki's secretary that I was going to the basement where the old books were stored and went down.

I was in luck and found nearly two hundred diverse titles waiting to be remaindered. Their covers had been torn off, which meant I could take them for free.

'Take your time,' said a familiar voice. 'Even the philistines have their uses because they don't read.'

I turned and saw Janaki Bose, our humanities editor, behind me. She was poking into a pile of very dusty books. I knew what she meant. Some very fine books went to the pavement shops straight from the cartons in which they had arrived from England.

Ms Bose was about thirty years my senior in age, and rather more than that in experience. Everyone was scared of her, even Nikki who was our boss. It wasn't 'scared' as out of fear but 'scared' because of awe. She simply knew far more than any of us and made sure that we understood that by rarely speaking, even at meetings. But when she spoke it was the final view. I avoided her as much as I could. She, I felt, regarded me as a typical product of my class. It was only much later that I realized how wrong I was.

Eventually, after about an hour or so, I collected

twenty-four novels and one non-fiction title. I realized this was the first tour I was going on after Sunidhi's departure. Before that, I would have picked out four or five books on subaltern history, post-modernist painting, antipodal anthropology and other fake subjects. It was relief not to have to. The non-fiction book I found was on dogs, called *Man Meets Dog* by Konrad Lorenz.

Oddly, though, Sunidhi had no interest in, or ear for music. I was quite good at it myself even though I could not play any instrument. Even more oddly, we never quarrelled about it. We went for many concerts but she would spend a lot of time chatting to friends in the foyer. The same thing happened with my radio and the Phillips record player she gifted me. She never made any requests about what to listen to or play.

I found a peon to put the books in a carton and carry them to my car where he placed them in the boot. Then I went back up to my office and asked Mrs Singhal to write letters to the six authors saying I would be calling on them next month.

'When they reply, please tell the fellows in the travel department to make the rail bookings and inform our reps as well,' I told her. Then I went home to plan a strategy.

I had absolutely no idea how I was going to persuade these superstars to write for us. My only chance lay in convincing them, through the power of suggestion and other forms of deception, that their books would be published out of London. Then I would see if I could

show their books on my Indian list. The time had come
to stare down the Empire. I would need the managing
director's help and fully intended to ask for it. But
if they insisted on a London job, I would at least be
able to argue that I had found the superstar authors
to publish with us.

• • •

I was not senior enough to fly. But as a 'covenanted
officer' I was entitled to First Class Ordinary or
Second Class Air Conditioned by rail. Not many trains
had air-conditioned coaches, so it was on First Class
Ordinary that I was booked to travel to Ahmadabad,
my first port of call. The professors in question taught
at the management institute there. One was an expert
in marketing, the other in monetary policy. Both were
in their late thirties. Both were stars in that they had
published a lot. I had to land one or both of them
for my list. The quality of the manuscripts was not
a problem. They could submit utterly mediocre stuff
and they would still be accepted. That's how the star
system worked.

The travel department had booked me on the
slowest train it could find. It left Delhi at eleven at
night and reached Ahmadabad the next evening at
nine. During the day it traversed the Rajasthan desert,
very slowly, and stopping frequently.

'Don't drink on the train,' Mala Auntie cautioned
me when I went to say bye to them on my way to the
station.

'Yes, but you can drink now,' said Mike, handing me a large tumbler of whiskey filled halfway to the top. Mala Auntie looked disapproving but said nothing.

I remembered that I had not asked her about her manuscript.

'Any news, Auntie? Of the book, I mean?'

'Not yet. I am making some corrections. You will have to get it typed again, I am afraid.'

We sat down for dinner and by the time we got up I had had another large drink. It was far more than I usually drank. But, as I would discover in a few hours, not so good as to prevent a severe headache brought on by the heat on the train. Like all trains, it had been parked in the sun through the day and was baking inside even at midnight. I had forgotten to bring some water along and by three in the morning I was ready to die. Being a slow train it stopped every half hour or so but none of the wayside stations where it halted had water. This was, after all, the desert of Rajasthan or very near it.

Around six in the morning we finally pulled slowly into Jaipur. The sun had been up for half an hour and a hot wind was blowing across the platform. I bought a surahi, filled it and drank three surahis-full. Slowly some sense of the normal returned. Then I stood under a huge water spout that was used to fill water in steam locomotives. The force was enough to make me hold on to the railing nearby. Then seeing that there were still fifteen minutes left for the train to get going again I went to the dining room for the

First Class passengers where I ate the huge omelette with liberally buttered sweet bread that the railways specialized in. The tea was sweet and milky enough to qualify as a barfi. The air was so lacking in humidity that by the time I came out of the dining room, I was completely dry.

I thought I would complain against the fool in travel who had booked me on this ridiculous train. No wonder I had been alone in my six-berther first-class coach. It even had a tub for ice because the Brits had had the good sense to cool the coaches with 50-kilo blocks of ice that melted as they went along and which were replaced from time to time. After independence, the practice had been given up as being too decadent. Now the tubs were filthy because no one cleaned them. The only solace was the attached bathroom with a shower from which very hot water trickled out. I kept wetting my shirt to remain cool and threw it away later that evening. It was only later I realized that Sunidhi had made me buy it, saying I should stop wearing only white khadi bush shirts.

We left at six-thirty. I felt fully restored because I had taken another shower under that giant water hose just before the train pulled out. I pulled out a book to read but in less than twenty minutes the train was baking. And in half an hour I was lying flat on the berth wishing I was dead.

We lurched moodily on through the desert, all three hundred miles of it at 30 miles per hour. Just after five in the evening we entered Gujarat. The landscape turned greener and slowly by about six the temperature also started to come down. I hadn't had anything to eat the whole day so when the train stopped at Godhra, I bought a huge platter made of some local leaf with eight bondas on it. A small boy turned up with some warm bottles of Coca-Cola and I bought six from him, enough to see me through till we reached Ahmadabad around nine. I also filled my surahi from the tap. The bondas were a mistake because very soon I finished the water. Then I drank the Cokes and that made things even worse. If there was a hell on earth, this was it.

We eventually reached Ahmadabad at nine forty-five, not very late by the elastic standards of the Indian Railways. Our local sales representative, Govind Bhatt, was waiting at the platform. He was a tall, thin man who spoke with a lisp. He had been with the company for two decades, he told me, and had not been promoted even once. I felt odd when he kept calling me 'Sir'. I asked him to call me by name. He took me to the hotel where we had dinner in which everything tasted faintly sweet.

He gave me a brief description of the books scene in Gujarat. 'Nil. Zero. Gujaratis don't know English and don't want to learn it. And because they don't buy English books, I have not been promoted. In fact,' he added moodily, 'they don't read at all.'

I felt sorry for him but thought he was exaggerating. He went off at about eleven saying he would be back at ten the next morning. I went up to my room, showered, ordered some sandwiches from room service and ate and slept.

• • •

The meeting with the economics professor started quite badly. First he asked why he should give his manuscript to us. Then he asked how much royalty we would pay and demanded double the standard rate. Then he refused to have his work refereed, saying that no one in India could evaluate his work. Finally, he wanted a guaranteed sale of at least two thousand copies, two-thirds in the UK and US. All this before he had even told me the name of his book.

Even though I had no authority, I agreed to all his demands. If I could get him formally signed up and on my list, it would give me a reason to plead for a postponement of the evil day. It would also give me a chance to tell the company that they could not treat stars and dogs on the same footing. They would howl in anger and pain. But I knew that in the end they would agree after issuing me a written warning for having exceeded my authority. Persuading London after that would be their job, not mine. If London said no, we could say it was their fault; if it said yes, my stock would go up. I had it all worked out.

With some difficulty I managed to persuade the professor, an Oriya called Santosh Mahapatra, to show me his manuscript. It was 600 pages in double-spaced typescript which meant roughly 1,00,000 words or 300 pages end to end. That would give me a unit cost of

12 with the charts and tables for 2,000 copies. This meant a minimum price of 60 per copy. With the author's premium added on I would suggest a price of 100 and agree to 85.

The company wouldn't make much money but this was the Catch-22 of publishing. To keep cover prices low, you printed more copies but selling them all was not easy. You were fortunate if half the print run was sold and you made a small profit. It was a high-risk business dominated by the middlemen or distributors who kept asking for ever increasing discounts. Publishers compensated for it by cheating the authors of their legitimate royalty by wailing that hundreds of copies had remained unsold. The only sucker in the game was the author.

It was only after I had quickly done the sums that I looked at the title and introduction. I can't say I followed much of it but did manage to grasp the central point, which was that the government had erred badly by taking control of the price of money. The current orthodoxy in India was the opposite. It took some courage to say that everyone else was wrong but Mahapatra seemed quite unafraid. I knew instinctively that this was a winner and decided not to let go whatever happened. I would need Nikki's full support, though. Immediately, there was nothing more to do than give a verbal commitment to Mahapatra, which is what I did and left for my next meeting, a few rooms down the corridor, with the marketing wizard who had a PhD from Harvard and a string of publications and consultancies in the US and France.

The contrast with Mahapatra, who was short and intense, could not have been sharper. Professor Swami Narayan was tall and laid back.

'Hi,' he said, 'please call me Swami. And welcome to this house of mirrors. Is this your first time?'

I told him it was my third.

'So how is the fishing?'

I told him I had had a very successful meeting with Mahapatra. 'Almost signed him up, in fact.'

He grinned, looked at his watch and asked if I would like to wander down to the cafeteria.

'It will start filling up soon for the morning break, and become very noisy. I have a class immediately after so let's go and drink something.'

He bought the tea and led Bhatt and me out to a verandah reserved for faculty.

'This way the students can't hear us bitching about each other,' he said.

We settled down into enormous cane chairs around a cane table with a glass top. It was still very cool and the grass smelt nice. A very persistent crow was ranting on about something. I once again thought about the missed profession. Academics had it good, I thought.

'Right, okay, well,' said Swami, 'We have twenty minutes. So tell me what you want and I will say yes or no.'

I told him and he replied that his book was about something which Indians still did not comprehend.

'It isn't about selling, or marketing as they call it now. It is about the effects of competition on firms.

But in India we don't allow much competition. So we don't really know anything about selling in highly competitive markets. My book will flop here.'

'Flopping or not has nothing to do with the contents,' I told him. 'It's all to do with marketing.'

'Touché. I deserved that. Well done. Now tell me that you want me to do next?'

I asked him if I could take a look at the manuscript and he said yes.

'But can you go through it in my room, please, while I am in class? We can discuss what happens next over lunch.'

It became clear once again that I had a bestseller in my hands. What Narayan had done was simple. He had applied economic theory to the oddest of things and come up with a set of ideas that would, if nothing else, make for great topics of conversation in both business and economics faculties. For not having come up with the idea, both would call him names but that was his problem. As far as I was concerned, the book was by a star and it would sell.

I decided to offer him a signing advance. The company frowned on this but I would take a chance. I had nothing to lose but my job. This one would sell five thousand copies if the price was low and the price would be low only if it printed at least three thousand in the first run.

Over lunch I told him we would pay him 50 per cent of the estimated royalty when we signed the contract. He nodded and asked me if I had the papers for him to sign. I told him I would send them in a week.

'Thanks,' he said. 'I should be able to send you the final typescript by the end of the year.'

My luck seemed to have turned. It looked as if I had achieved two-thirds of my task on the first day itself. But I knew overcoming the enemy within was going to be much harder. There would be haggling over content, the length of the book, the print run, the price and the royalty. At every stage I would have to battle with the nit-pickers in editorial, the doomsayers in accounts and the cynics in marketing. Every editor faced this problem.

It was a strange system where someone was hired for his or her expertise and then opposed at every step. The idea that only accounts and marketing had the company's interests at heart and editorial was the enemy made no sense at all. But that's the way it was. I was convinced that I was paid so much for winning against the internal odds.

We talked about other things. I told him about the risks publishers took.

'Every book is a new product. Each has to be sold differently. And you never know which title will sell and which one will flop. Out of every ten thousand titles published worldwide, only one makes real money. Around half just cover the investment and the rest lose money for the publishers.'

He told me that with better marketing techniques these ratios could be changed. He asked me what the publicity budget for each book was.

'Three thousand rupees,' I said.

'Double it and see what happens. Spend some time and money on learning how to sell,' he said looking at his watch. 'Got a department meeting at two-thirty,' he said and was gone.

The rest of my trip, which involved looking for run-of-the-mill monographs and textbooks, was a complete washout. I went to half a dozen universities in as many towns and drew a complete blank. It was extraordinary how the Indian system of higher education had removed all incentives to publish anything by way of books and research. My last call was on the third star, a Bengali called Ajit Bose at, of all places, Waltair, a lovely little town on the east coast. The university had been built in the small hills that rose up from a couple of kilometres inland. Bose was a choleric fellow in need of Isabgol. He flatly refused to write for us.

'I publish only with university presses,' he said. That being that, I caught the evening train to Madras, indulging myself a bit more after my luxurious two days in the small hotel on the beach.

In Madras, which was my last stop, I told all this to the friends I was staying with. Both taught law at the university.

'Ours have always been teaching universities,' said Kamini, who had been in college with me. 'They are not research universities.'

'Promotions are not based on research but seniority,' added her husband, Ram. 'Degree factories is what we have created. You are more likely to be successful if you went hunting for textbooks.'

'Oh, I do that too, all the time' I said. 'It's part of my brief. But the problem is quality. These fellows draw up the syllabus, then write the textbook around it and prescribe their own books. Since each university has a different syllabus, we don't get All-India text books. Those have to be imported, and are expensive. So the students rely even more on cheaper local textbooks. It's a nice little vicious circle.'

'Perfectly rational, too,' Ram said, 'because if you write the answers from your professor's book, you can be sure of better marks.'

It was even worse in law, they told me.

'The instruction is case-law based so all you need to pass with decent marks is to read summaries of the main precedents. These are mass produced and cost next to nothing.'

In short, we concluded gloomily, all we had were guide books. Research and monographs were simply not needed for career progression, either for students or for the teachers. The incentive structure, as economists called it, was all wrong.

Kamini asked me if I could help her get her book published. She said it was on the Constitution but what she had written was not kosher. The Establishment would not countenance it.

'I think we have a pretty bad Constitution from our needs point of view. Why else would it have been amended forty-five times? It tries to do too much. It needs to be made to do less,' she said. 'People keep quoting that silly Latin thing *Si fractum non sit, noli id reficere* which means "If it ain't broke, don't fix it". But it *is* broken, always has been.'

'The US Constitution has been amended only 33 times in 227 years. The Australian Constitution has been amended eight times in 116 years, and it takes a referendum to get it done. The Irish Constitution has been amended 33 times in about 75 years. The French have made about 30 amendments in 56 years but most of these are about their colonies and elections, etc., not about administrative problems.'

Ram tried to restrain her from launching forth on a diatribe but he was too late. She got off to a terrific cold start. I had never seen anyone so animated and so agitated over so arcane a subject, not even Sunidhi, who could work up quite a froth over such things.

'An ill-favoured thing, my Lord, but mine own,' I said to her at one point but she ignored me.

'It is a fine document from an aspirations point of view,' she said, 'but it is simply not a practical one for a politically independent India. It suffers from two flaws. Its purpose is a colonial one, that is of a very strong central government and it gets into too much detail of the administrative kind. This has made conflict between the executive and the judiciary inevitable, even on matters that did not have any bearing on individual rights and freedoms.'

She raged on for a while more until Ram's and my silence forced her to stop. I asked her for a copy of the manuscript which she said she would send. I promised to find her a publisher. Maybe even our own formidable Ms Janaki Bose would look kindly on it.

• • •

I had planned my trip such that I would get the weekend in Madras so that I could visit my aging grand-uncles, who had brought up my father after his own died when he was just eleven. I did that over the next day and a half and then caught the train back to Delhi.

I had been away for nearly three weeks and impatient to get back home. I boarded the Tamil Nadu Express, just a few years old at the time, at ten at night. The railways had given me a lower berth in the second-class air-conditioned coach in a cubicle that didn't have any other passengers. I had the space all to myself and after reading for a while, I drifted off to sleep.

I became aware sometime around two that the train had stopped. I peered out of the window. We were at some wayside station. Since such stoppages were common, mostly to let some other train pass, I went back to sleep. But when I awoke a few hours later at around six and looked out of the window I realized that we had not moved at all. I got to my feet, drew the curtains of the cubicle aside and saw a young couple sitting on the two aisle seats, facing each other, and looking very unhappy and uncomfortable. They hadn't been there when we had started in Madras.

I asked them if there was a problem and the man said the tracks were under water a bit further up the line and that we were being diverted along some other route. He said, with some fury, that his parents who were to have got on at Ongole would now have to catch some other train, maybe a week from now.

I went out and got off the train. Except for the hum of the generator car, there was no other sound. I walked up and down the length of the train hoping to see someone from the railways but there wasn't a soul to be seen. I badly wanted some coffee and found the dining car where some cooks and waiters were just waking up. They said they'd be along in about an hour with coffee and tea.

It was noon by the time the train started again and took the long way. The man who came to check our tickets said the track was under water for about fifty miles and that the detour would add twelve to fourteen hours to the journey if all went well, which it didn't, of course. At one point, we stopped for three hours in the middle of a dense forest. It was early evening and very beautiful except for a million bugs that were returning home for dinner or setting out for it. A few hundred of them flew in through the open doors of the coaches and things became very uncomfortable for a while.

We finally reached Delhi twenty hours behind schedule, in the middle of the night, and in pouring monsoon rain. The food on the train had run out long ago and I was, like everyone else, hungry and angry. I eventually managed to find a taxi and reached home around two but couldn't sleep because I had done nothing except eat, read and sleep for thirty-five of the last forty-three hours. So I unpacked, cleaned the house a bit and sat for a while on the verandah, smoking.

Throughout the trip I had wondered if there would be a letter waiting for me from Madhavi. I opened the office packet that Mrs Singhal had sent over. There were two letters from her, one addressed to the office address and the other to the home address. I opened the latter eagerly only to find a short note thanking me for everything.

'Hope the project turns out well,' she had written. 'I expect to have the revised manuscript ready by the end of December.'

Disappointed for no reason, I turned to the rest. They were the usual stuff which I began putting to one side because there was nothing I could do with them at home. Towards the bottom of the pile I found the second envelope from Madhavi. It contained a three-page letter. She had sent the wrong envelopes to the wrong addresses. After re-reading it nearly half a dozen times, and I wrote a long reply that ran to four pages. I told her everything that had happened on the trip. If I had the necessary stamps, I would have posted it immediately.

It was almost dawn by then. The heavy rain had given way to a light drizzle. Feeling very pumped up because of the letter from Madhavi and also mine to her, I decided to go for a spin on my bike. I whipped down the wide road that connects Vasant Vihar to the Inner Ring Road and, after crossing the Moti Bagh bridge, I turned right at the roundabout and stopped at the two kiosks outside Chanakaya Cinema that were open all night for the taxi and auto drivers. Two cups of hot sweet tea, hot buttery buns with a hot three-egg omelette inside, two cigarettes and some desultory talk with a couple of policemen later, I drove back home and immediately fell asleep.

A few hours later I was back at work.

• • •

Nikki's response when I told her about my trip was like the one that greets a centre-forward who misses a goal by a whisker.

'Two isn't what we agreed on. It has to be three. I can't shield you this time. But anyway, tell me more.'

I did, and she became very angry when I came to the financial commitments I had made to Mahapatra and Swami. I knew why she was so furious. It was not because the authors were not big enough for such promises to be made. It was because it was impossible to resile from them without seriously harming the company's reputation. No author was promised what I had promised Mahapatra and Swami. There had to be proper discussion, a recommendation by the committee and the managing director's approval. If at all, only Nikki was authorized in the rarest of rare instances. At my level, which was the juniormost, it was cause for strict disciplinary action, if not dismissal.

She had been raging at me for about five minutes when Mrs Singhal came in to say that there was a call for me. 'It is very urgent,' she said with an uncharacteristically worried look.

Nikki, who had stopped in mid-sentence, nodded at me and said, 'I will see you after lunch. Please prepare a written explanation in the meantime.'

I returned to my room and found the phone on the hook. There was no call and I turned to go back to Mrs Singhal to ask where the call was from but found her standing right behind me.

'Would you like to dictate that note now,' she asked. I did and the storm blew over, for the moment at least. I still had to find the one missing star, though.

• • •

On 14 August, Mike and Shiv turned up with three girls. One of them was Jyoti. I wondered why she was here with Mike if she was getting married in a month's time. Mike told me.

'The fellow got cold feet,' he said. 'AC/DC, it seems'.

I didn't ask him how he knew this little nugget but he told me anyway. 'Jyoti told me a few days back.'

She seemed none the worse for what is generally regarded as a traumatic experience.

Around midnight, Shiv said he would drop the girls off. Mike stayed on. We talked about Jyoti for a long time. This was the first time I had seen him like this. No lewd comments and no desire to get off the topic of Jyoti, not to mention the mixture of hope and wistfulness that spoke volumes. Before turning in he reminded me of his free ticket offer.

'I am on the roster for Thursday. Then I go on to

New York and will be back for a layover till Wednesday evening.'

I told him I would come along and went off to phone Debbie. She wasn't in. I told the operator to try again a little later. The phone rang again at two-thirty. Groggily, I asked Debbie if I could come over the next weekend and she said yes.

'The others will start coming back by the end of the month, so this is perfect.' She seemed genuinely pleased. I told her I'd find my way to her house and rang off.

As always, the week sometimes seemed to go by too slowly and sometimes too quickly. Nikki looked at me without any expression when I told her I had a free ticket to England and back and asked for a week off.

'I will get you some smoked ham,' I told her. She signed the leave slip.

As I was leaving she said, 'Find the time to meet Frampton. He seems to like you and will be offended if you slink off without saying hello. And before you ask how he will know you are there, let me tell you. You will carry a packet from me to be delivered to him personally.'

It didn't seem like too much of a bother, so I said I would. Frampton wasn't a bad sort, just a bit awkward with Indians who he thought hated the Brits. Nikki and the others had tried to tell him that we didn't mind them really but it was hard to convince him. He insisted on being embarrassingly courteous.

By the end of the day everyone in the office knew I was going to England on a free ticket. Around five that evening I was handed a long shopping list which I threw quietly into the dustbin. Some scotch for the men and a box of chocolates for the women would do.

• • •

Just before setting out for home, I got a call from Gibbsy. He said he was in Delhi on some sort of courier duty. Usually it meant going back and forth from the embassy to the airport and the junior staff had to do it. But sometimes they needed something to be sent to headquarters and the seniormost amongst the junior staff was despatched—with a briefcase chained to her or his wrist. I laughed at the thought of Gibbsy roaming around an airport like that and asked him to come over for dinner on his way to the airport. He said he would.

He brought along a bottle of scotch which we opened and drank slowly on the verandah. The lights had gone thanks to the power cuts caused by the shortage of electricity from the hydel plants. We were, after all, in the middle of a terrible drought. But there was light drizzle and it was very cool outside. It was also very quiet and we heard only the light rain. Just a few years earlier, we would have heard the monsoon frogs croaking but now they were gone.

I asked Gibbsy how Ro was adjusting to her new life in an Indian mission in the Middle East.

'Not very well, I am afraid,' he said. 'Those buggers impose too many restrictions on women, who are more-or-less confined to their homes when not accompanied by their husbands.'

I asked if these restrictions applied to foreign women too and he said no one was exempt.

'Pretty awful to be a woman there,' he said.

Even though it was only a couple of months since he had gone there, I could see he was worried. Ro was accustomed to having her way and these shackles were bound to annoy her hugely. I wondered briefly how long it would be before she blew a fuse.

As always Gibbsy read my thoughts and said, 'I have told her to return home and take up her old job while I am there. It's not too far away and she can come once a month. It will cost a bit but it might be worth it.'

'What about the other wives?' I asked.

He said the mission was small, with a staff of about fifteen people. 'Only three of us are from the senior branch of the Service. The rest are support staff and it's not easy to socialize with them. An informal caste system largely restricts the wives of the senior branch officers to their own type. It's a hangover from the British days when you didn't mix with the natives and other ranks.'

So Ro, he said, had the choice of the ambassador's wife, which was a complete no-no because of the huge difference in rank and age, or the first secretary's wife who wasn't much fun to be with. What he meant was that she came from a very different and wholly non-Westernized background.

I knew exactly what he meant. We had a couple of them in our office, attractive till they opened their mouths. We called them the 'hai pata hai' types. The more pejorative term was 'behenjis'.

I felt very sorry for Ro but there was nothing I could do. I changed to subject to his own work and from what he said, it seemed just like mine because he had very little to do.

'You know, at first we enjoyed going to National Day functions and parties at the homes of chaps from other countries. But even that has become a bore because you meet the same crowd, drink the same booze, eat the same food and complain about the same things. Only thirty-three countries have missions there.'

The rest, he said, blowing smoke at a lizard on the wall, had simply asked some other country to represent them, the Swiss being the most sought after. And even amongst those that have proper embassies, the staff exceeded twenty only in the case of the Americans. Worse still, most the wives had opted to return home.

'Ro is lonely and bored out of her wits. I think she will be back here sooner than she thinks,' he said.

He asked me how things were for me, post-Sunidhi. She had been very fond of him, and he of her. But he had warned me once or twice that she wasn't my type. She's too intense, he had said. I had told him he was wrong and that she was terrific fun. But in retrospect, he had read her better than I had. Or rather, we had both been right. Only, he had been righter.

I told him my problem was no longer Sunidhi but my office who had more-or-less served me notice. He heard me out and said I should have joined the government or the public sector.

'They sack you only if you go mad, or for something

called moral turpitude. Competence and diligence are irrelevant.'

I told him it was too late now and that I would have to make the best of it. We drank some more, had dinner, sat about on the verandah till his staff car came to fetch him at about eleven and he left for the airport. I realized, with a slight sense of misgiving, that I had forgotten to tell Gibbsy about my trip to London the next day.

I spent the next couple of hours cleaning up because I hate coming back to a messy home. Then I packed by putting everything in the cupboard into my suitcase. The bundle of socks in the lower shelf reminded me to look for my shoes. I had only one pair and having put them away in March when the weather started turning warm, I had forgotten that the heel of one of them had come off. I went to bed feeling very foolish and very irritated, and hoped that Mike would be carrying a spare pair. He usually did.

5

Mike picked me up at four-thirty in the morning in the office car and I boarded the Air India 747 at six without much fuss. Once the doors had been shut and we were on our way, a stewardess came and took me up to the cockpit which was on the second level in the 747, in front of the business class. She knocked on the door and Mike opened it to let me in. He pointed to the jump seat and I sat down there as we gathered speed and took off. It was an extraordinary experience to look straight up from the nose of a plane at a sky full of monsoon clouds, lit with flashes of lightning. About half an hour into the flight, Mike told me we were crossing over into Pakistan. A short while later a stewardess led me down to the first class section and a window seat. There were only three others there, all fast asleep.

'With the compliments of the airline, Sir,' she said. Mike had done his bit.

She brought me breakfast, an amazing five-course affair. It was only seven-thirty in the morning but she asked me if I wanted a drink. I did and she left a half-bottle with me. I had never had such fun in my life. No wonder Mike was addicted to this life.

Presently, I dropped off to sleep. It was past noon when I came to. There's no other word for it, so deeply was I asleep. Mike was prodding me in the ribs with his boot and asking me to come for another visit to the cockpit. 'We will soon be over the Med,' he said.

I told him I'd be along in a moment and went to brush my teeth and wash my face. The bathroom was another big surprise, full of all sorts of lotions and pastes and brushes. I put a few in my pocket but needn't have bothered. The stewardess had left a grey cardboard overnight bag with the Air India Maharaja on the cover on my seat. It was full of goodies, including some cognac.

I went up, opened the door to the cockpit and went in. The captain was asleep and Mike was in charge. I stood behind him and looked out at the sun-drenched sea below. There were hundreds of boats there. The white and coloured sails were clearly visible even from 33,000 feet. In the distance there were some islands and even further up, blue hills. The cockpit was very silent because the engines were far behind. All that was missing was the hiss of the wind in a glider. We were quietly floating above two thousand years of history.

From time to time Mike murmured into his mouthpiece and made very slight adjustments. It all looked very easy but I knew it was anything but. After about half an hour the captain woke up and said he would take a stroll around the plane. Mike motioned for me to sit on the vacant seat and for the next twenty minutes I saw the sky and the earth and the sea as pilots do.

Nothing I had ever experienced matched the serenity of that cockpit. Mike didn't talk and left me to absorb it all. The glare surprised me and I finally understood the need for those dark glasses that pilots are shown wearing. The captain came back and looked a little put out that I had been sitting on the most sacred seat on a plane. He took over the plane when we left Turkey behind us.

Mike and I went to the bar on the upper level. I drank some more vodka and then went off for another nap before we got to London. An hour or so later, I was back in the cockpit, watching the French coast come up. Being a World War II buff I imagined what it would have been like for those pilots as they flew back and forth across the Channel shooting at each other. I recalled reading a book called the *Eighth Passenger* by an RAF crew member. He said everyone thought there were seven of them on those Lancaster bombers but actually there was an eighth passenger which was, well, fear. It was one of the best books I have read about World War II. Only fools were brave; the others were just very scared.

I had once had a very heated argument with Sunidhi who was something of a Europhile. My contention was that for all their music and philosophy and art and architecture and so on, the Europeans had been pretty uncivilized, ready to fight on the slightest pretext.

'Much of the history of Europe and Britain is the history of fighting,' I had said and she had tried to play it all down because of some Marx-inspired nonsense about antagonistic classes. I had made the mistake of laughing and she had blown her fuse. It had always been like that: her truths were superior.

In a few minutes we were over England. Mike asked me once again to sit on the jump seat. On our right were the famed white cliffs of Dover. We landed at Heathrow about thirty minutes later after a great deal of going left and right and left again. Watching the two of them fly that mammoth aluminium tube quietly, bringing it down onto the runway with such deep concentration and focus, was absolutely extraordinary. They did it with such practised ease that I began to see Mike in a completely differently light.

I went back, fetched my goody bag and said bye to Mike who was standing at the door, smiling and mumbling inanities to disembarking passengers. We agreed to meet a few days later when he got back from New York at the hotel he had booked for me.

Unlike on my previous visit, this time it was a short walk to the immigration counter. The girl stamped me in without looking up. I looked at the queues of people from countries that needed visas and felt good that Indians didn't. I took the bus to Victoria and slept on another to Birmingham. A taxi took me to Debbie's home on Mostyn Road, which I reached at seven-thirty in the evening. Fifteen hours door to door wasn't bad, I told her when she opened the door and gave me a hug. I took the cognac out of the Air India goody bag and gave it to her.

The sun was still up and we went to a tiny restaurant

for dinner where we ate some Italian food and drank some of what they called their house wine. I remember the bill because I insisted on paying: four pounds. I left a five-pound note on the table and Debbie said that in England people didn't tip twenty per cent. 'Twenty pence would have been quite enough.'

She then took me for a drive around the city in her small ancient car which she said she had bought for fifty pounds from a student who had graduated. We went to see a film after that, a murder mystery from the 1950s. I slept through most of it. It was midnight by the time we got back. I was quite tired by then and went off to my room and had a glass of the whiskey which I had brought along. It was a gift from the captain, the stewardess had said.

It was a tiny room, no more than 80 or so square feet, with a large bed and a small desk and chair. There was a cupboard in the corner which took up a lot of space. The window looked down into a small garden with a couple of benches and tables. There was a tree right in the middle of the garden—an apple tree, it later turned out—and a birdbath under it. It was what I had imagined such places to be like from all the books I had read about England.

But as often happens if you shower before sleeping, I lay awake for a long time thinking maudlin thoughts. The fact that it was still light perhaps had something to do with it. Or maybe it was the unaccustomed stillness or the lingering smell of fresh paint. Perhaps it was all the alcohol I had drunk in the last eighteen hours.

Whatever it was, I had a strangely unquiet mind that evening and it was only after I had figured out what was bothering me that I finally slept.

I realized that I had pushed the question of Sunidhi to the back of my mind. Almost the first thought that had crossed it after I told Mike I would come along was whether I would see her or even phone her. It had been nagging me for the last week. I just could not decide because I had no idea how she would react. Our last meeting a year earlier had been a strange one.

It was already two years since we had gone our separate ways. I had run into her at a mutual friend's house and she had introduced me to her current love. He seemed a decent enough fellow and was obviously completely unaware of my relationship with Sunidhi. She had left me with him and ignored me completely after that. I made some excuses and left a short while later.

A couple of days later she phoned and asked me to take her to see a play at Pragati Maidan near the river. 'Vishnu has gone to Bombay,' she said. I should have refused but didn't. It felt nice and natural and comfortable to be there with her. I think she felt the same way.

We went for dinner to York's in the outer circle of Connaught Place because I knew they served liquor there even though Delhi was under prohibition. The whiskey came in teapots and was drunk out of teacups with saucers. Sunidhi had had a cup too and became slightly giggly. After dinner, I had driven her over to where she was staying.

We sat without talking for a few minutes before she got out. Then she said, 'Well, then, goodbye. I don't suppose we will meet again. Be good and stop wasting yourself. Read a good book or something.' And then very quickly she was gone.

I had driven home furious with her but had got over it by having several quick flings with girls looking to cock a snook at their parents. I had thought less and less of Sunidhi over the last year or so. But now the question had to be faced.

I decided finally that I would stay away. She didn't know I was in England and wouldn't have cared even if she had.

• • •

It was a little past eight when I woke up next morning. I went down to the dining room and kitchen. I had no idea how it worked. Debbie was not up yet but her fat Labrador, John, was asleep on the rug. He looked at me and banged his tail on the floor a couple of times. Debbie later told me that anyone coming down the stairs was fine with him and that he barked only when strangers came in through the front door.

So I let myself out into the garden and waited on the bench for Debbie to descend, which she did about half an hour later. She came out barefoot with two mugs, tea for her and coffee for me. I congratulated her on her powers of observation.

We sat there for a long time talking about nothing in particular. She told me about her nomadic childhood and I told her about mine. The one thing that emerged was that we hadn't made any long-term friends from school.

'Shall we drive up to Cambridge,' she asked at one point. 'If we leave at ten we can have lunch there and go around the colleges afterwards. It's only about a hundred miles away. The colleges really are very lovely, especially King's.'

So that's what we did. Cambridge was truly stunning and I wished I had made the effort to get a scholarship there. We did the usual things, a walk along the Backs, crossed the Mathematical Bridge, inspected the King's College chapel, and at my request, climbed up to see where John Maynard Keynes had had his rooms. Debbie showed me her college and told me about how once there was a fire drill and many boys had come popping out of the rooms.

'It doesn't happen only in the movies,' she said.

On the way back we returned via Newmarket and had supper there at a McDonald's. I had wanted to see it because of all the Dick Francis horse-racing mystery novels I had read. It figures prominently in them because it is the so-called capital of the British horse-racing world. It was a drab place, nothing much to see and I apologized to Debbie for making her go there.

It was late evening when we got back to Birmingham and Debbie suggested we go for the weekly Friday open-air music performance. 'Today,' she said, 'it is by a local pianist and it is free.' So we went there.

Someone was selling very red apples and wine and

cheese cubes at the entrance. We bought some and sat on the grass and ate and listened. I thought of the times I had been to concerts with Sunidhi in Delhi in the winter of 1975 and 1976. In spite of my decision the previous evening, the unresolved question was still there. Should I call her while I was here? There was no easy answer and it still lurked just beneath my consciousness when I went to sleep that night.

The next day was Saturday and in the morning Debbie said we could drive to Oxford. 'My boyfriend lives a few miles out and we can have lunch with him and then go into town.'

The boyfriend, a doctor, lived in a large converted barn. The structure was exactly like a haveli in Rajasthan. The living room was the entire ground floor and the bedrooms were above on the sides. But the bathroom, just one in true English fashion, was downstairs. I thought of telling them about Versailles palace which had almost a hundred rooms and no bathrooms but stopped in time. I had read somewhere that the Louises used to place large tureens on the ground floor and pee into them from the top. The historian had not said what the women did. But he did say that the French royalty and aristocracy built so many homes because without proper bathrooms and sanitation, the stench became unbearable after a while. In India, the sun acted as a super disinfectant but snakes and scorpions were a problem.

Oxford turned out to be far less pretty than Cambridge and somehow rougher in its demeanour.

Maybe it looked better when the sun was out. Debbie took me to the all the usual spots for tourists. On one street I saw a sign at the entrance to a church saying second-hand books were on sale in the basement. We went down to take a look and it was absolutely wonderful. Everything was for a pound. I bought seven books, including one by Percival Spear who had taught in some Delhi University college for a long time. The odd book was for Debbie who couldn't make up her mind whether or not to buy it. It was E.M. Forster's *Passage to India*.

On the way back she told me that she usually visited her mother on Sunday afternoons. I said I would leave for London by noon. We spent the evening in companionable silence in her sitting room. Then we went to our respective beds. Neither of us thought we'd be seeing each other again. There was some sadness but not much. I had taken her to Dehra Doon and she had returned the favour by taking me to Cambridge and Oxford.

It was quits.

• • •

On the bus to London the next day, I manfully wrestled with the Sunidhi question once again. Truth to tell, I desperately wanted to see her even though I was sure I didn't love her any more. But she remained in my head like an unidentifiable sound, irritating and desirable in equal parts.

I no longer thought of her all the time. Nor did

I resent her when I did think of her. I had stopped writing to her a long time ago but the need to speak was strong.

She was a bad listener and was given to hectoring in a censorious manner. She was very judgmental about certain people and things and ideas and suspended judgement completely on other people and things and ideas. Morality was what she thought it was, not fixed or absolute. An opinion was correct not because it was based on facts but because it was held by someone she admired intellectually. Logic for her was a substitute for low cunning. Her love for me notwithstanding, I never qualified in that regard.

Contexts mattered at times and didn't at others. The underprivileged were right by definition and the privileged were wrong ab initio. She thought nothing of splurging huge sums of money on her birthday and then crying when she came out of the restaurant and saw a child begging. She flew between cities and took buses once there. I told her that it was better to either take trains or buses between cities and taxis after reaching there. She got very annoyed and didn't speak to me for a week. Or so it seemed then.

Confrontations were to be avoided with everyone except me, and those tended to be fierce, intense and prolonged. I had to be there when she needed me but a request for the reverse was an infringement and abridgement of her sovereignty. The books I read were trash. The jokes I told were vulgar. The work I did was all right but did I have to do it so badly? All things

considered and regardless of how much I loved her—
and she me—she could be a pain in the neck.

I am sure she thought the same about me. For her,
I was a kid who could not be abandoned, who needed
intellectual nurturing, and tutorials in compassion and
empathy. And, of course, my manners were deplorable
which I daresay they were. I thought nothing of helping
myself to the best portions of food, the best chairs
wherever we went and the first rights on everything,
from newspapers to books to you name it.

'You have been brought up altogether too feudally,'
she would insist.

So everything considered, I should not have
bothered with her after I had got over the initial shock
of rejection. And yet, here I was, on a bus to London,
wondering if I should call her, knowing that I could
well be brusquely told that I shouldn't have.

She had done that a few days after I had dropped
her off after the play. I had called her on an impulse
and regretted it so much that I had sworn, come what
may, never to speak to her again. But the tussle went
on nevertheless. Perhaps it kept my mind occupied on
tedious journeys. Perhaps by not calling her I felt I had
somehow 'won' in the end. Maybe it was like worrying
a rotten tooth with your tongue, both nice and awful
simultaneously. I didn't think I would ever find out.

The bus eventually reached London at three in
the afternoon and I took a taxi to Tavistock Square
in Bloomsbury to stay the night with my friend Arun
who was now an economist at the London School of

Economics. We had been in the same class. I had passed only because of his notes and tutorials.

The next day, I was to move into a hotel where Mike had got me a good rate through his airline. They used it for the cabin crew. The pilots and engineers stayed in much greater luxury.

'Even at half the rack rate, you can't afford it,' Mike had said.

• • •

Arun asked me if I'd like to listen to a talk by a learned bishop from Canterbury or just stay home and watch cricket on TV. From the way he asked, it was evident that he wanted to go for the lecture, so I said cricket could wait. The lecture was at five so we sat around for bit talking about Margaret Thatcher who had been elected prime minister two months ago and then took the Tube to the venue.

The hall was packed but we managed to find a place to sit. A few minutes into the talk and I was itching to have a go at the pompous bishop. The burden of his song was that Western notions of morality, because they were absolute and did not depend on the context, were superior to non-Western ones which all too often did. Arun, too, was looking annoyed. In the end we decided not to say anything and left as soon as the man finished.

'There's a nice pub close to my place and we can go there for dinner,' Arun said.

It was very crowded and we had to wait for a

while before finding a table where I waited, while Arun fetched the beer. The music was loud and it soon seemed pointless to stay on if we had to shout to be heard. Pubs, obviously, were places of catharsis for the English who were otherwise a very glum lot.

Arun was apologetic when we came out. 'I forgot it was Sunday. I never go to pubs on weekends.'

'Context,' I said, 'seems important for how even these prigs behave.'

Arun smiled and apologized again. 'I would not have gone but my girlfriend insisted I attend.' Et tu, Brute, I thought to myself.

We bought some food at a Pakistani shop and went home. Arun phoned his girlfriend to ask if she could come over, which she did presently. She taught politics at London University. Her name was Angie. She was a rather large woman, in her early forties, I guessed. She was wearing an ankle-length skirt of the medieval sort, a kurta that needed a wash and kolhapuri chappals. She said she had been to India half a dozen times in the last three years because of Arun.

'Delhi, Bombay, Calcutta, Madras, Nagpur, Nasik, Bangalore...you name it, I have been there.'

That evening was, in some ways, the high point of my visit. Arun and Angie seemed perfectly matched in their preferences. They were solicitous to each other in the way that batsmen, who have played a lot alongside each other, take quick singles. The understanding was in the quick glances, the slight nods, the little gestures. They didn't need to get married, nor did they need to live together. Perhaps that was the mistake I had made with Sunidhi.

It was well past midnight when we drifted off to bed. Angie said she would stay the night. Just before I turned off the light in my room, Arun knocked and came in.

'I saw Sunidhi a few days ago. She asked about you. Do you want to meet her?'

I said nothing. I just looked at him. He stared back.

'Oh, I see. Okay, good night then. Angie will go off by seven so if you want to say bye to her, you'd better be down by then.'

• • •

Our office in London was not far away and next morning I decided to walk the four-odd kilometres. It was a beautiful day, cool and crisp, blue sky, yellow sunshine, the sort of morning which always fills me with pleasant nostalgia. I had told Frampton I'd be there by eleven but reached with about half an hour to spare.

I hadn't had any breakfast, so I went into a Wimpy's which was nearby and bought an omelette and a glass of milk. I was the only customer and I quietly watched Londoners go by. They all seemed preoccupied and worried. They hardly seemed to speak. I had read somewhere that the difference between Europeans and Americans lay in their walk. Europeans sauntered while Americans walked purposefully. It was nonsense, of course, but the writer had said it was this difference that had helped the police spot Victor Lustig, the man who sold the Eiffel Tower. Lustig had sold it not once but twice! Both times to an American, naturally, though not the same one.

I found Frampton at his fussy best. He shook hands, sat me down, asked his secretary to get some tea, looked for a pair of scissors, carefully cut open the Sellotape on the packet and gingerly took out the contents. It turned out to be a manuscript, a rather large one, nearly one thousand two hundred pages of foolscap sheets typed in double space. I had no idea whose it was.

Looking quite pleased, he put it aside and looked up. He was looking older than his forty-six years. The grey suit was crumpled and the shirt collar just slightly soiled. I wondered why he dressed so formally if he wasn't going to iron his clothes. I had noticed many locals who wore unironed shirts, suits and ties.

We talked mainly about his list and what he thought we should import. By the end of the hour that he had allotted to me he had given me a list of nearly fifty titles. He wanted me to make sure that the fellows in marketing ordered at least a hundred copies of each. At an average price of ten pounds, that came to a fifty-thousand pound order. There was no way this was going to happen in a single order. Over three years, perhaps. But not at one go.

I told him as much. 'Monographs don't sell very well in India.'

He became a little tense. 'Please do what you can,' he said. 'Nikki will help.'

I left without promising anything. This sort of thing

was not up to me, anyway, and if Frampton needed to impress his bosses, he would have to use someone else. I also wondered why, for such a large order, the big guns hadn't gone into action. All they had to do was to tell the managing director in India and it would be done. In any case, I had my own problem to solve, namely, find that elusive third author.

I had nothing more to do now except wait for Mike. He was due in a couple of hours. I decided to walk back to Arun's flat to pick up my suitcase and go to the hotel. Arun was still around and we drank some beer and ate some bread and cheese and tomatoes. He asked if I would like them as a sandwich and I said separately was just fine. He gave me a short lecture on sandwiches and their history, etymology and use.

'In a restaurant it's cheaper to eat them separately than in their value-added form as a sandwich,' he said. 'That's why you can't order them separately.' His class was at four and, in true Indian style, he went off to take a nap.

The hotel was on a street just off the Thames Embankment. I checked in and went for a walk. Then I waited in the lounge for Mike to turn up. It was almost three by the time he came.

Sunidhi came with him.

• • •

'Look,' said Mike angrily, 'she insisted. She was on the flight and saw me and asked about you. I said you were in London. I shouldn't have but it just slipped out. Sorry.'

'Oh, do be quiet, Mike,' Sunidhi said. 'Go away and fly a plane or something.' She turned to me. 'The bar is open. Come.'

Mike looked at me, furious with himself and with Sunidhi. He saw my expression and went off in a huff. Sunidhi looked at me and smiled.

'Mike will be Mike. Always defending and protecting you. Let's go for a walk. I need to stretch my legs after that long flight.'

'What do you want, Dopes?' I asked when we had crossed over to the riverside of the road. I had started calling her that because of her large dopey eyes, not unlike a Beagle's.

'Nothing,' she said. 'I have to wait for Jeremy till eight. When Mike told me you were in town I thought it would be a pleasant enough way of killing time.'

I looked at her. She looked tense. I knew that light-hearted, casual tone only too well. She got it when she was hiding something.

'Okay, so tell me about him. Has he turned out to be a disappointment, too?'

She didn't reply. Instead, she perched herself on the parapet and looked obstinate. So I asked her again. This time she replied.

'Yes. But not in the way you turned out to be one. You were the opposite. You were very clingy.'

I waited for her to continue. If he was my opposite, by definition he had to be the most preferred fellow around.

It took her a long time to come out with it. 'He has been sleeping around.'

I thought it was a bit rich coming from her. She had always held that love and sex had nothing to do with each other. Casual sex was just that, casual, like going for a film or a concert or a drink with a friend. Not that she had ever indulged in it or would. Deep down she was a prude as well. But theoretically, speaking from the point of view of the human spirit, in the context of male dominance...

I had pointed this out to her once with the usual result, a week-long sulk. At the end of our little quarrel, she had given me a book called *Praxis* by some French Marxist. Broadly, it meant the interface of theory and practice. That, at least, is what I thought it meant. It was one of the first things I threw away after she had dumped me.

'And you haven't? Is that the problem?'

I was surprised at how offhand I was being with her. I could see that she was seeking some form of solace and I was being obnoxious instead.

She told me not be cheap because, she said, it wasn't the *me* she knew. 'Vulgar, always, but cheap never. Unless it's something you have picked up recently.'

I looked at her. She was wearing her usual sari, a silk one, perhaps one I had got her, I didn't remember. It was a nice orange one. She was tall and was able to carry herself well even though she couldn't manage to tie them quite as elegantly as so many other women did. I had asked her once to learn the tricks from a friend of hers who was very good at it and, of course, she had gone into a sulk. Her hair was neatly pinned back for the flight so I leaned over undid the clip. It fell around her shoulders. She didn't seem to notice what I had done and I must say I too was a bit surprised that I had done so without thinking.

She was staring at a boat going by. But the look on her face was that faraway one that came when she was about to start crying.

'Don't,' I said. 'I will walk away if you do.'

She called me a rude name in Hindi. 'I don't know what to do.'

'Confront,' I said. 'Confound. Compel. Confuse. All the things you are so good at.'

It was a strange afternoon that we spent together. We talked about things that were intensely personal to her. Her dumping me never came up. It was as if she didn't think she had dumped me. She seemed to think I would always be there when she needed me. I felt strangely gratified at being taken for granted like this. But it was also annoying.

I, for my part, mostly listened, occasionally prodding a reply or explanation from her.

The half hour Sunidhi had promised Mike turned into several more. We went back to the hotel and sat in my room. Mike had a couple of drinks and went off to his fancy hotel, saying he would see me on the flight now on Friday night. I thought Sunidhi would leave but she didn't. We had dinner and she decided to check into a room. 'Jeremy can stew,' she said.

So it was still about him and I was just a useful fellow to have around. I should have made my excuses and left but didn't. I didn't know when we would be like this again, if ever. I also realized that I had fallen completely out of love. Her departure hurt still but only the ego, not the heart. So we talked well into the night, side by side on the bed because in cheap hotels like this one in England they give only one hard, straight-backed chair. Once she asked me to massage her neck which I did. It was just like old times, except of course it wasn't.

She told me about her work, her colleagues, her parents, her brother, her friends, and her lows and highs. There was something that had changed. When she had left India eighteen months ago, she had been a very trusting sort of person who took everything and everyone at face value. But now, from what she was saying, she was beginning to question people's motives. Although she wouldn't admit it, she was also hinting at the film of racism that permeated England. She also said she had begun to learn the subtleties of English speech and how they tended to invert the meanings of words.

'It takes you a while to understand what they really mean,' she told me.

I mostly listened, wondering why she was telling me all this, dreading that she would ask me what I had been up to since we last met. I decided not to tell her about my several flings. But I don't think she would have cared. She seemed to see me as a very good friend from back home, who would be gone the next day, and who would probably never be seen again or at least for a very long time. It was a strange feeling.

It was as if she was trying to create a new person out of me, and change the reasons why we had been such good friends.

'You have changed, you know,' she said at one point. 'You don't talk very much any longer. Earlier you used to go on and on, mostly about yourself.' I told her my brain had become very dull because of the amount of whiskey and vodka I drank these days.

'What happened to the charas?' she asked. I had got her to smoke some once and she hadn't forgotten how hungry it had made her. I told her charas was no longer available as easily as it had been before. Nor was it as cheap. The Emergency had changed that market forever.

It was two in the morning when she finally went back to her room. I slept soundly for the first time in months, or even years, relaxed, content and free. She had said she wasn't coming back to India. I felt strangely relieved. I no longer felt like pandering to her emotional needs which were always intense, varied and several. It had been good while it lasted and bad when it was spluttering out. Now it was like a stuffed bird or tiger, dead but yet somehow alive, when you look and wonder, gosh, this thing had a life in it once.

Then, just before I dropped off, the word came to me: catharsis. I had had mine and I rather hoped that she had had hers as well.

We had breakfast together the next morning in the dining room. She was looking moody and depressed, so I read the paper instead. We didn't talk at all and a little later Jeremy came around to fetch her. They went off in his car. I felt sorry for her. She had embarked down a road that was unlikely to give her much stability and if there was anything she needed to be at her brilliant best, it was a stable environment. She tended to fret a lot and when she fretted she could not focus on her work, which made her fret even more. The cycle continued till it all blew up one day in one almighty row. The problem was she needed someone to blow it up on, with or at. I wondered if the Jeremys of the world were the answer.

• • •

The next four days went by quickly. The weather was nice, the days long and my mind light. I did the usual tourist rounds and marvelled at how much the English made of so little. India was infinitely older and richer in terms of monuments and the like. But the English carried on as if they'd invented history. Much of it was because of their obsession with preserving all sorts of things and re-inventing them if they happened to start disintegrating. Much of the Tower of London was new, or restored, as they liked to call it.

But the British Museum was a genuine treat. It made me feel, alternately, angry, elated and depressed. The scale of English loot was unparalleled in history but their dedication to preserving the things they had stolen more than compensated for their greed. On balance, and anger notwithstanding, I thought this was better because we kept things very carelessly in India.

I thought of the time Shiv and I had gone to see the stupa at Sanchi where some of the Buddha's remains are supposed to be interred. The electrical fittings outside the entrance were in a complete tangle. Shiv had asked the caretaker about it and had been told that they had indented three years ago for a new junction box. It had yet to arrive. In the meantime, if there was a short circuit, the whole edifice could be badly damaged—or perhaps not. It was carved out of stone in the third century before the Christian Era started. There was nothing to burn there.

In the evenings I went for plays, live concerts and walks in the City. I was perfectly content to be by myself. This too was a change that Sunidhi's departure had caused. I had lost interest in friends, small talk or big, and generally in other people's views and opinions. Gibbsy, perceptive as ever, and an expert on the brain, had once told me in his gruff way that I was on the verge of being clinically depressed. I had no idea what he meant.

On my last evening I called Arun to see if I could take him out for dinner. He asked if Angie could come too and I said yes. We went to a Greek restaurant and got into a long argument over Britain's legacy in India. I said it was good. Angie said it was bad. Arun said it was a bit of both. As always with such bouts with words, no one learnt anything new and nor did anyone emerge wiser. I knew none of us would even remember what we had said for longer than an hour. Later, when Angie had gone round the corner, he asked me if I had met Sunidhi.

'As it happens, yes,' I said, 'we talked.' And then I changed the subject. She and I had a private relationship that would remain private. I am sure she also kept her side of the unspoken bargain. In a sense, we were like a couple who had divorced after a decade of marriage.

My flight was at eleven the next evening but the hotel wanted me to check out at noon. I asked how much they'd charge if I kept the room till six. They said a full day's rent. I mentioned this to Arun who said to come over by ten because he had to leave by then.

'I will be back by five so you don't have to waste your money.'

So that's what I did. The London School of Economics wasn't very far away. I walked to it and spent a fruitful morning at the famed bookshop there. I bought a book for Shiv on the politics of oil since the mid-nineteenth century and the diary of Churchill's personal physician, Lord Moran, for Ms Bose. It had caused a minor controversy when it came out over patient confidentiality. Lord Moran had said that for much of the war Churchill was physically a wreck, ill from a heart attack and a stroke. How can people trust a man so unwell during such a critical period, he had asked. Many Brits had cursed him roundly for being so rude.

Then I bought some bottles of wine and whiskey for Arun and the Brigadier and some creams and suchlike for Mala Auntie. It occurred to me then that I should have bought her a book as well. So I went back to the LSE and bought her one. It was on justice, a topic she would often talk about after reading something in the newspapers. India, she said, had all the means for dispensing it but never actually got around to doing it. The Brigadier, in his precise way, said it was like a bathroom with no water. The shop girl gave me a discount when I said I worked for a publishing firm and mentioned the name. It wasn't much, just ten per cent, but it was a nice gesture.

Back in the flat while waiting for Arun to return, and against my better judgement but out of some residual concern, I called Sunidhi to see how she was getting on. Jeremy picked up the phone.

'She's gone,' he said. I asked if she had left a number. He said no and rang off.

Goodbye, Jeremy, I thought. But was it also going to be goodbye, Sunidhi? Later, on the flight, when he joined me for a drink Mike said I was looking different somehow. I didn't tell him that I was feeling different too.

It was only after we had crossed over into Russia and I had had what seemed like a dozen whiskies that I thought of Madhavi and felt a frisson, the first since I had met Sunidhi five years ago.

6

It had not rained at all in England for the seven days I was there. But it was pouring hard when we landed in Delhi. Once again I was in the cockpit watching the goings-on as we floated down from 35,000 feet to the ground. It took almost an hour. Mike showed me how that gigantic machine was lined up with the runway. The two of them landed the thing without being able to see anything in front. Even after we were down, the only thing visible through the sheets of water on the windscreen was the dim pilot light of the tow vehicle as it guided us to our spot opposite the terminal.

The buses were drawn right up to last step of the ladder so that we could step straight into them. That would take time for the fifteen bus-loads. But I was once again in first class and Mike had shooed me out when we came to a halt. So I got to the terminal quickly. It was chaotic there with wet floors, crowds, too few immigration staff and no luggage trolleys. It took two hours of shifting from leg to leg, darting between carousels for my bag and an angry exchange with a chap in a uniform for a trolley—he was from Customs, he shouted back angrily—before I came out.

It was still raining hard. The water was up to my ankles. My suitcase, a very old leather one that had belonged to my grandfather who had bought it in Zanzibar or some such place, was soaked. I feared the handle buckle would give way. Eventually, balancing my suitcase and the gift hamper from the airline, I found an auto-rickshaw to take me home. He charged six times the normal fare even though my home was barely five kilometres away. Nothing like India to bring you down to earth, I thought, as we waited for another thirty-five minutes for a flooded road to clear. The worst part was that my last pack of cigarettes had got sodden.

I hadn't been able to tell the newspaper boy before I left to stop delivery and found around a hundred pages of soggy newsprint clogging the front steps. I kicked them aside and remembered that I had forgotten to take the front door keys out of the suitcase where I had put them while away. Annoyed, wet, tired, hung-over, it was at least four hours after landing before I found myself back inside the flat. There was nothing to eat because I had emptied the fridge before leaving. I tried to call the shop but the rain had knocked out the phone.

There was nothing to do but wait for the rain to stop. I put some water into the fridge, showered and got into my shorts and T-shirt and sat down under the fan, wondering what to do next. Then I remembered the gift hamper which contained two half-bottles of vodka and whiskey, a shortcake and a huge bar of chocolate.

'Enough unto the day,' I said to myself and to the

accompaniment of heavy rain outside, drank myself into a deep sleep with vodka, biscuits and chocolate.

It was well past noon when I recovered consciousness. I drank some ice-cold water and went out to the verandah. The hard rain seemed to have stopped but there was still a steady drizzle. So going anywhere was probably not possible. The phone was still dead so calling for food was also not on. I was wide awake and enormously hungry. I found a cigarette packet in one of the drawers, lit up and wondered what to do.

In the end, there seemed no alternative but to walk down to the local market. When I reached it around two it was shut except for a man selling eggs and buns from a cycle rickshaw. I bought eight of those for the price of ten, ate three on the spot, and took the rest home for later.

For the next three hours I sat on the verandah, smoking, sipping whiskey, reading and thinking about my problem. The trip to England had been a useful interregnum but that's all. I had to find the third star author or resign. I had two hundred and ten days left. Fifty-six of those days would be weekends and another seven holidays. That left just about a hundred and fifty days.

I wondered briefly if I could commission an anthology to be edited by some big-shot Indian. But good though the idea was, there was no way it could get done in a hundred and fifty days. I then wondered if I could try and put together unpublished papers of some star. But the ever-present problem of London grabbing the volume remained. Besides, who knew if anyone had three hundred pages worth of unpublished papers? I cursed the star system. I raged for a while asking who decided Dr X was a star and that Dr Y was not, even though he or she was every bit as good, if not better. I sympathized with Shiv who would have to play the game or sit it out for the rest of his life. Knowing him it would probably be the latter.

Finally, I decided to try out an idea that had been forming in my mind ever since I had met Frampton. If he wanted a favour from me to save his job, why not get him to do me one as well to save mine?

It was then that the penny dropped. Nikki had known about Frampton's problem all along. That's why she had insisted I see him. She must have calculated that, despite my seemingly naïve approach to life, I had enough low cunning to work out the logical quid pro quo. In fact, she must have asked Frampton to ask me because otherwise, from his point of view, I was too junior a cog in the machine.

But she could not choose the books without consulting me. Procedure was procedure. Nikki had probably told him that 'proper procedure' required that only if I recommended the books could she approve them for import. That's the problem with 'proper procedure'. It can work both ways. Even then the marketing fellows would have the last word on it. But I would fight that battle later. Immediately, I had to work out how to get Frampton to come to the aid of the native.

I spent of the day pottering about. Later in the afternoon I went for a movie because there were bound to be some food stalls there. I wanted to save the bun-omelettes for the night. I suppose I could have brought some food back from the theatre but the bird-in-the-bush thing prompted me not to take a chance. It was a good decision. The food stall was closed and the movie was rubbish.

I left halfway through it and went for a long ride on my bike. I had always wanted to go right around the Inner Ring Road to see how long it would take. I drove past Dhaula Kuan, down the newly widened road to Naraina, up the flyover there and down into a new colony which was stupidly called Punjabi Bagh, past Azadpur, Model Town, Kingsway Camp, Rajghat, Ashram, AIIMS and RK Puram. I was back at home in Vasant Vihar in exactly fifty-two minutes. But for a small holdup near Azadpur where a bus had broken down, it would have been even less. Had the roads been dry, perhaps even less than that.

It was only after I got back home and settled down on the verandah that I started thinking about how small Delhi really was. And because it was small, even little changes were highly visible. One of the things that was changing was the accent in which Delhi spoke. Earlier it used to be Punjabi. But now it had become the guttural one from Haryana. When I had mentioned this to Shiv one day, he had muttered with some annoyance that soon it would be the Bihari accent that characterized Delhi most.

I sat there thinking, on and off, about Madhavi and wondering about taking her for a ride in the rain one day. I continued doing that after eating the fruit I had bought from a drenched stall-owner near AIIMS who had charged me double, I think. I realized a little while later I could have easily gone to Mike's house for dinner, as I would have done even a few weeks ago.

Things, it seemed, were changing, the old pulls were weakening, new ones beckoning, possibly to no result but it was something else to think about, if not look forward to. And that is what I did for the rest of the evening sitting out on the vernadah, drinking, smoking, watching the rain vary its pace, glad somehow that I was in a state of complete detachment and contentment after so long.

• • •

Despite having gone to bed only at around two-thirty I woke up, as always, just before daybreak. Sundays for the past two years had become something to be borne with fortitude, an unwelcome interruption of the process of mindless barging about. I found some old milk powder and scraped out the coffee from its jar. There was still some sugar sticking to the sides of its container and I poured boiling hot water into it. Then I dropped the coffee and the milk into it and drank a wonderfully sweet brew straight from the jar. The sky had cleared and a cool breeze was blowing. I again sat on the verandah waiting for the milkman, the car cleaner and the newspaper boy. They came, and by eight life had returned to normal, only to be shattered half an hour later by the clatter of the gate.

I looked up from the newspaper and saw it was Shiv. He was beside himself with rage and shouting incoherently. I had never seen him in this state before, so I just sat and waited for him to calm down. He went to the spare bedroom, dug out a towel, went to the bathroom and came out after about half an hour, bathed and calmer, if not calm. He helped himself to two bananas, ate them at a furious pace, drank some water from the fridge and sat down opposite me.

'I am going to kill the bitch,' he said. 'Why don't you have any tea or sugar? I have almost finished your milk, so you'd better tell that fellow to get you some more. I am going to kill the bitch,' he said again.

'Good,' I said. 'When, where and why?'

The full story came out eventually. Shiv said he had been up for the assistant editorship of the department's history journal, by all accounts a well regarded publication. Since it was the assistant editor who wrote to everyone, it was a great platform from which to wave your arms about to be noticed by the glitterati amongst historians. It was what the doctors ordered for a twenty-eight-year-old budding academic with airs.

But it was not to be. 'She' had slipped in one of her protégés for the post.

'God knows when I will get another chance,' he shouted. 'I will kill the bitch,' he said for about the tenth time.

The sun was out, the breeze had dropped and it was getting uncomfortably warm. Torrential rain or not, it was still Delhi in August. I told Shiv to get some beer from somewhere while I arranged lunch. He went off and came back half an hour later with a case from somewhere. I wondered why he couldn't be as resourceful when it came to his work. Delhi was, after all, under prohibition and this was a superb demonstration of his skills, contacts and powers of persuasion.

Mala Auntie called when he was away and asked me to come for dinner. I told her Shiv would probably be around and she said to bring him along too.

'I like to see you boys,' she said.

Over lunch Shiv told me about the work he was doing. It seemed pretty good even to my untrained ears. I asked him whether he could produce a quick book of about two hundred and fifty pages.

'A book published by us would look good on your bio,' I said.

He said he had enough material for a collection of papers but not an entire book on a single theme. I told him to bring the lot to me so that I could show them to Ms Bose.

'She will know if they are any good or not.'

Shiv looked a little doubtful but I managed to persuade him and after lunch we drove up to Shiv's rooms where he dragged down a box from on top of a bookshelf.

'There they are, all the buggers, arranged date-wise from the bottom.'

I asked him if he had copies and he said yes. I left soon after and went back to sleep. Shiv came back at around seven and we both drove to Mike's house for dinner which turned out to be the usual pleasant affair.

Mala Auntie told me she was done with the changes and corrections in the manuscript and handed it over to me for retyping. The Brigadier said he had started yoga. Mike said he was off to Tokyo in a few hours and would come with me to my flat till it was time for the office car to fetch him. I told them about my trip and about Cambridge and Oxford and Birmingham and all the rest.

Shiv just drank steadily without saying much.

• • •

'So you figured it out. Good,' said Nikki the next day as we stood smoking on the balcony. 'Now take a good look at Frampton's list and pick out whatever you want, one, two, three, ten authors. We will have some fun now. They have it coming to them.'

As always happens when you come back to the office after a break, you somehow expect things to have changed. But they haven't, of course. Life has gone on exactly as before without you.

I had given Mrs Singhal the perfume I had bought for her and left the rest of the stuff with her to be distributed to the other ranks. Then I had gone in to see Nikki who seemed genuinely pleased to see me. I started to tell her about the trip but she held up her hand.

'Later,' she said. 'On the balcony. I am expecting a call from the MD. He wants to know what we are doing. That Brit who was here has been complaining.'

I knew who she was talking about. Frederic Winters, known as the Big F in the company, was very high up on the accounts side in London. He met only the MD who was also an accountant and would complain that we in editorial were not up to the exacting standards of London. He used to come over twice a year. Once was in August, to combine his summer holiday with company business to save on the air fare and half of the hotel bills. The next trip out was in March, just before the financial year ended. The March trip was very short, just a couple of days but the August one would drag on. Making Delhi his base, he would go to Sri Lanka, Singapore, Nepal, Bhutan, the Maldives, Indonesia and what have you.

Our chief accountant, an upright and easily scandalized Tamil Brahmin, had told me once that he would find ingenious ways of charging his private stays to the company. In effect, the Indian shareholders were paying for his Lordship just as the Indians had done when the Empire still existed. It was some fiddle with the discounts on one or two consignments that we imported.

I went back to my room to look through the accumulated mail. By eleven, when the tea boy came around, I had disposed of most of it. Most of it was routine anyway which Mrs Singhal would take care of. I only signed. But there were around half a dozen which needed non-routine responses, including one each from Swami, Mahapatra and Madhavi.

Nikki was waiting for me on the balcony. She closed the grille door behind me and bolted it. Clearly, something more than just a 'how was the trip' chat was on her mind. For the first few minutes, though, that was how it went, with me telling her about the cockpit and the English countryside and suchlike.

'Frampton was on the phone on Friday,' she said finally getting down to it. 'He sounded very anxious that you would not give him his orders.'

I told her that he wanted a fifty-thousand-pound order.

'But he told me twenty-five thousand,' she said. 'But never mind. He will be happy with ten now. Those guys have landed the company in a hole and now are looking to their overseas subsidiaries to bail them out.'

'How will a mere ten help?'

'Actually, they are looking to get around a hundred thousand from us over the next three years. Then there are all those others in the rest of the world. All told, their target is a million or thereabouts. Everyone has to come to the rescue. England expects and all that.'

'And they expect that everyone else will agree, just like that?'

'Well, they are realistic enough to see that there will be a price to pay. I doubt if they will sell any shares to raise the money but other ways can be found.'

'Like what?'

'I am not entirely clear. Last week when you were

away, the MD had the department heads over to tell us what was going on. Play it properly, he said, and we can't get what we need to become big on our own, without their support.'

'What's all this got to do with me?'

'Nothing just yet but who knows? Anyway, you'd better get that third author signed up quickly. Winters had to postpone his vacation and will be here in October.'

She told me to keep all this to myself and went back to her room. Despite the light drizzle that had started, I stood around for a bit longer, wondering who was playing at what. My immediate task seemed simple enough: to recommend the import of titles worth ten thousand pounds over the next three months.

I needed some advice and after racking my brains for almost two hours, I had a brainwave. I would ask Mrs Singhal how I should use the opportunity. She knew from the secretaries' grapevine that I was one short, as also that my job depended on finding the third author by March.

After lunch I asked her in and dictated the replies to Swami, Mahapatra, Madhavi and the rest of them. Finally, when we were done, I asked Mrs Singhal to arrange for two cups of tea and when those had come I explained the problem to her.

She looked surprised that I was asking her but recovered very quickly.

'Simple,' she said. 'Ask them to transfer one of their authors to you. We publish here, they buy from us, and not the other way around. After all, they have taken a few from us, no?'

My respect for her went up because this was exactly what I had thought I would do. Had her circumstances been different, she would have been doing something far more important than merely typing letters for almost forty years for a series of upper-class twits. I thanked her and she left.

I knew it wasn't going to be just a matter of picking out an author and saying, 'Right, Frampton, I think I will take this one, if you don't mind.' Frampton would fight, as would his boss. It was going to be a very enjoyable little tussle, with Nikki and I on one side and Frampton and his boss, a woman called Sarah Benson, on the other.

Nikki and Sarah, who was close to retirement, were constantly in conflict over volumes and discounts. Nikki thought Sarah was a sales type who had been dumped on editorial. Sarah went about saying Nikki knew nothing about publishing. Since copies of all letters written the previous week were circulated for information, we all saw their barbs in the letters they exchanged. The two of them kept it civil, but barely.

Feeling very pleased with myself, I started riffling through London's forthcoming list. They had almost five hundred titles coming out between October and April. Around a third of these were in economics, finance, management and accounting. I found the last three subjects utterly boring and focused on economics. Of the hundred and seventy-three titles that Frampton and his gang were overseeing, forty-three were on pure economics. Only two were stars. One of them was an Indian but his book was on an arcane aspect of economic theory. Marketing would reject it outright.

The other star, however, had written on India but she was English. Her name was Bridget Sampson, Professor, Oxford University and Adviser, HMG's foreign office. For all these reasons marketing would agree to sell two thousand copies. Subterfuge would be needed with Frampton because I needed to see the proofs. The saying about not judging a book by its cover is a hundred per cent right. I had discovered this in my first year. An American star had written rubbish on the global oil economy and we had been left with a few hundred unsold copies. It happens to everyone from time to time, Nikki had said and added, 'Caveat emptor.'

I called Mrs Singhal in and dictated a letter to Frampton thanking him for seeing me and so on. I didn't mention anything else. Let him stew, I thought. Then I picked up Shiv's bundle and went across to Ms Bose. I gave her the book I had bought for her. She looked genuinely pleased.

'Thank you so much. I have heard so much about this book.'

We chatted about England for a while. She said she had been at the Cavendish Laboratory for a year after she had finished her post-graduation.

'Lovely place but freezing,' she said. 'All that wind down the Fens.'

Then I handed her Shiv's papers. I told her about him and that he was a close friend.

'Just see if they amount to anything and if they can be published.'

She said she would in a couple of days and I went back to my room, signed the remaining letters, popped my head into Nikki's room to tell her I had found my third star but she had left for the day. Pleased overall with the way the day had gone, I drove back home feeling content in a way I had not for close to two years. Only one thing remained to be done, a letter to Madhavi telling her about my trip.

I wrote twelve pages.

• • •

September in Delhi is a strange month. The summer begins to give way to autumn but very gradually. It is also the month when, thanks to the abundant sunlight and the rain of the previous month, the vegetation proliferates even in the cracks in walls. The moisture in the atmosphere is just right and in combination with the heat, all kinds of viruses flourish. The water supply of the city being what it is, sewage often seeps into the drinking water, so water-borne diseases have a field day. A former India captain who I used to see about his autobiography once told me how, despite living in a posh colony, he had received a letter from the municipality that this had happened and that they should boil the water till further notice. He was much impressed by this sense of responsibility on the part of the municipality till his wife made the mistake of pointing out the date on the letter. It was forty-five days old.

So it did not come as a surprise to anyone that by the second week of September, half the office was bed-ridden for one reason or the other. In editorial, only Nikki and I were spared. Ms Bose was down with dengue and the science editor with jaundice. The rest were out of commission on account of a variety of illnesses. Amongst the secretarial staff only Mrs Singhal was present. So she stood in for all the rest without fuss, which led Nikki to remark that perhaps they could be let go. The same thought had occurred to me as well.

The office was very quiet with twelve of the thirty people missing. I wondered if I should go off on another tour, this time to the smaller towns like Bangalore, Hyderabad and so on. But Nikki refused to let me go, instead asking me to handle the routine work of the others. She and I talked a lot about all sorts of things and I was once again amazed not only at how truly well-read she was but also at how sensibly she had sorted out all the facts and analyses.

She tended to look at everything from an anthropological viewpoint. Individual behaviour for her was boring, only group behaviour mattered.

'It's like that utility thing you economics types go on about. You can't add up every individual's utility and say right, chaps, here's what social utility looks like. It doesn't work that way, not in economics, not in sociology nor in any human endeavour.'

One day, to break the tedium in the office, we decided to go out for lunch. I took her to my club. On the way I asked her what her husband did. In the four years she had been my boss, the topic had never come up. To me her private life mattered so little that I never thought about it. In fact, once out of the office I hardly ever thought about anyone in it. Office was yet to become the only thing in my life.

'I don't have one,' she said. 'My boyfriend died before we could get married. Bike crash. On the Ring Road. Near Rajghat. Fourteen years ago. He was going home after dropping me off. We had been to see a film in CP. He ran into some steel rods jutting out from the back of an unlit bullock cart. He didn't see the cart till it was too late and one of them went right through his heart.'

She said it with the dryness of someone who has narrated the incident many times. She said she had never been able to get over him because of the suddenness with which it had happened. Sudden departures of loved ones for no good reason were the hardest to get over, I thought, even if the loved one was still around in one piece.

After we had ordered, she asked me if I had any girlfriends. I told her how the trip to London had sorted out one of the two major complications.

'You are lucky,' she said. 'I just can't seem to stop feeling sorry for myself.' I said nothing even though I had a PhD in feeling sorry for myself.

We started seeing a lot of each other after that day because it was the silly season in the office, even without the illnesses. Eventually we ended up in bed, two lonely people and all that. It happened on a Saturday and we spent the entire weekend together at her flat off the Deer Park. Afterwards, she seemed quite casual about it which made me feel awkward. I wondered masochistically and with some futility if she had done this earlier. She probably had.

'This was a one-off thing,' she said later. 'Don't boast about it.'

'I am not that sort of boy,' I said and we went out companionably for dinner at the Golden Dragon and a film at Priya.

• • •

The reply from Frampton came after the usual two weeks that even air mail took. He sounded a little plaintive and demanded a response to his request. I wrote back saying I was taking it up with the marketing department and would get back to him after the customary market surveys had been done. That meant at least four weeks more. Then I added a postscript. Could I take Bridget Sampson on to my list?

I took the letter to Nikki before I signed it. She said it was fine but changed marketing department to managing editor.

'I will take three weeks to scrutinize and then marketing will take four. It will be mid-November by then. He should get sufficiently frantic before we agree. Anyway, Frampton knows the procedure. Let's see if he gets the message.'

Mala Auntie's revised manuscript had also come back from Mrs Singhal, three copies neatly retyped and bound. I spent an entire afternoon reading it and found that she had changed the ending. The novel had become less depressing as a result. It was a very slight change, just the deletion of the last five paragraphs. But it was amazing how just that little left the reader feeling optimistic and good. So very Mala Auntie, I thought.

I took the file to the literature editor, a round woman in her mid-fifties called Aruna Swaminathan. She was back from her illness, and looking none the worse for it. When only the two of us were there, she always spoke to me in Tamil. Once, when I had asked her why, she said she loved to hear my Tamil. It is so awful, she said.

Her name for me was Idiot Boy in Tamil, muttal-paiyyen. In retaliation, I called her Mami. She had told everyone in the office that she was looking out for a nice girl for me. I was slightly wary of her, not only because she was almost twice my age but also because there was a strong chance that she knew one or more people in my family. She could also see right through me and I wondered how long it would take her to guess about Nikki and me.

'Aah, muttal-paiyyen?' she said in Tamil. 'What do you want? And thanks for being so efficient with my mail. You are a good boy.'

'Hello, Mami,' I replied also in Tamil. 'Feeling okay now?'

She asked me to sit down and sent for coffee. 'I am

ninety-nine per cent okay,' she said, 'but the indigestion from all those medicines is troublesome. But before you tell me what you want, paiyya, tell me, will you come to my place to meet a girl this Sunday? She's working on her PhD in Bombay. My niece actually, North Indian Tamil like you, twenty-eight years of age, so a bit long in the tooth as these things go. She meets all your requirements, including the all-important one of despising her own clan, caste, tribe, their rituals and, of course, the Indian cultural heritage. It will be a perfect match.'

I said I would, most certainly, why not, but would there be lunch? I will not come at five in the evening for tiffin, I said. She seemed a little taken aback by my ready acceptance and told me to come the coming Sunday.

I slid the typescript across the desk to her and told her it was by someone I knew very well.

'Will you let me know if it is any good and suggest a publisher?'

She said she would and as we waited for the coffee, she told me that London was getting very troublesome.

'They want me to add five titles to their list, can you believe it? They have started something called the South Asian Studies Series and are now scrounging for manuscripts.'

We moaned about London for a while longer and then I went back to my room. It was getting on to five-thirty and in a few minutes everyone would be gone. Nikki had sent her car to the garage which had said it would take the entire week to fix. So I was ferrying her between office and home. She normally stayed on till about six-thirty.

By mutual consent and understanding there had been no repeat of that weekend. Nor had we referred to it or felt the need to do it again. Perhaps we were just waiting for the natural moment to arrive. A bond had developed between us, the sort that comes with shared experiences and secrets. It was the kind of thing one finds between school and college friends, a disappearance of natural barriers, an unselfconscious openness about the most private feelings of every sort, from fear and happiness to the urge to complain about parents and siblings. I don't know if the others noticed the altered chemistry and dynamics between us. I kept away from her just as much as I used to before, so perhaps there was nothing much to notice. But women have a sixth sense about such things and I worried about it, as I am sure did Nikki. And Mrs Singhal was shrewd as they come, in the same class as Aruna.

A few days later Ms Bose came into my room and said Shiv's papers were really very good and that she would send them to a referee for the usual reasons.

'There is no real need, I think,' she said, 'but I suppose he will have to go through the hoops and rings like everyone else.'

The next day, it was Aruna's turn. She came in and sat down and said Mala Auntie's manuscript was really top class.

'It's a pity we don't do fiction.'

'Why don't you send it to London,' I asked. 'You know, South Asian Literature and all that?'

'Good idea,' she said. 'But if you have another copy, send it to this man.' She handed me a slip of paper with a name and address on it. 'He is a connoisseur of good writing and sharp stories. Small but highly effective.'

I asked Shiv to come over to Mala Auntie's house that evening by seven-thirty and told him to bring along some good whiskey and a case of beer. Then I phoned Mala Auntie and told her I would bring some food. She didn't ask why because we did this once or twice a year.

• • •

Sunday came around and I looked for something appropriate to wear to Aruna's house. She had warned me not to turn up in my usual white khadi bush shirt and grey cotton trousers. 'I don't think my niece cares but her parents might.' I asked her what the niece was called and was finally given a name, a rather nice one actually, Vidya.

I must say I was most pleasantly surprised on all counts. Aruna lived in Jor Bagh. Her house was much larger than I had expected. There was a garden. There were two cars in the drive. The drawing room had two window air conditioners in it. There was beer on the table, and kebabs and, above all, there was Vidya who seemed friendly enough even though she must have known why I was there. She was of middling height, had a longish face and very long hair that almost came down to the hem of the pista green kurta she was wearing on top of her jeans.

'Hello,' she said when Aruna introduced us. 'I have heard a lot about you from my aunt.'

We opened the beer and settled ourselves down on the sofas. It was all a little awkward even though Vidya kept up a steady prattle. I asked her about her PhD and she said it was on the relationship between editors and proprietors of newspapers in India.

'You know, as an undergraduate, my father used to make to me read *The Statesman* because he said it would improve my English. Reading the editorial page, I used to often wish that I too could be an editorial writer.'

She told me how after MA she had been selected for just such a job. 'Pure luck,' she said. 'I worked there for three years, you know. Once or twice a week I would write an editorial and the editor would always re-write them.'

That, she said, was her first lesson in the business: the editorial was the personal view of the editor, although the fiction was that it was the view of the paper or journal.

'Much is made of the collegiate approach. People usually believe that the editorial is the considered view of a group of talented intellectuals. Nothing could be further from the truth. It is the editor's view, pure and simple. We just did the drafts. The thing is no more than a very pretty vanity.'

She got up to refill my beer and asked if I would give her a cigarette. I lighted it for her and she took a deep breath with her eyes closed tightly, loving the smoke that went in so quickly and out so slowly.

'My first smoke in two days, would you believe it. And I normally smoke twenty. My aunt makes a lot of fuss.' I told her how she chided me at least three times a day in the office.

I pressed her about her job and she said the morning editorial meetings used to be solemn affairs, leavened only by some snappy gossip about who was doing what and where and to whom. She looked at me with a question in her eyes and I nodded to say I knew what she meant.

'Then about fifteen minutes before the meeting gets over the editor asks you, "So, what are we going to say on this?"'

'You know, at first,' she said, 'I thought the man really wanted my opinion. But it soon became clear that what he was really saying was "say something with which I can agree". As ego fulfilment went there were few jobs like being the editor. It's all about power.'

One of the things she had discovered was the systemic flaw which made an institution that was regarded as being an integral part of democracy, liberalism, freedom, etc., itself be subject to the worst forms of dictatorship and tyranny. This was because under Indian laws, the editor had absolute power over the journalists.

'That's what my PhD is on,' she told me. 'There are no fetters, other than self-imposed ones, on the editor's ability to do exactly as he or she pleases. There is no court of appeal. That many editors are neither tyrants nor dictators is not the point. It does not detract from the systemic flaw. And it certainly lays newspapers open to gross abuse.' It was autocracy at its purest, she said.

I asked her if something needed to be done to reduce the internal powers of the editor.

'I guess so,' she said, 'but that requires a change in the laws that govern journalism. I doubt if anyone is bothered enough.'

It was getting on to two o'clock by then and kebabs notwithstanding, I was becoming hungry. The three glasses of beer I had drunk were making me drowsy. She saw me glancing at my watch and said Aruna would be down soon. She was busy giving lunch to her mother who was confined to a wheelchair after a fall in the bathroom had damaged her hip.

Sure enough, Aruna came in a few minutes later and started organizing the lunch. It was an elaborate affair, as befits an occasion when 'boy has come to see girl'. I counted nine dishes and six side things in smaller bowls. There was nearly a ton of rice or so it seemed.

I asked Aruna if the 'girl' had cooked everything as she is meant to on such occasions. She told me to think whatever suited me. Vidya said she had made the sambhar and the rasam. A few minutes into the meal, the front doorbell rang and the maid ushered in a chap of about my age. We were introduced. His name was Vinay Khullar and Aruna said, somewhat testily I thought, that he worked for a bank.

We ate on, but I could sense the tension around the table. Aruna was being extra solicitous to me, as she was expected to be, I suppose. But it was her manner to Vinay that stood out. Indeed, there was no manner or manners at all. She ignored him as completely as anyone can ignore a guest.

He was a decent enough chap but not the kind I would have automatically befriended. Vidya chatted to him with a fair degree of warmth and tried to make up for Aruna's offhand manner. I watched their dynamics and Aruna watched me watching them and when Vidya had gone into the kitchen to fetch something, she said loudly in Tamil that 'this fellow is hanging around Vidya'. It was said rapidly, in a normal tone and without any change in inflexion. I said nothing. What could I have said, anyway?

It was almost three by the time we finished. I wanted to go home and take a nap. Vidya and I had got along well enough but there was no spark, as they say. I got up to go, thanked Aruna for a splendid Tamil meal, said bye to Vinay and went out. Before I could shut the door Vidya came out behind me.

'Well,' she said, 'it was nice meeting you. Thanks for coming. My aunt has been very persistent and I guess she can tell my mother that she has done her bit.'

I asked her about Vinay and she said they had been going steady for two years and that no one in her family knew because both of them lived in Bombay.

'He came down for the weekend to see how I was.

We are planning to get married when I submit my thesis. I was wondering if you'd tell Aruna that one of these days. After all, you see her every day.'

And that was that. I rode away, a cigarette dangling from my lips, thinking about Madhavi.

7

The festival season was looming. The puja break was for five days between Wednesday and Sunday, if you counted the weekend. For the first time in two years I didn't feel resentful of the holidays that the season brought along. Mike suggested a drive into the hills in his new car, which he had actually purchased second hand from a French diplomat whose tour of India had ended. It was a jeep-like thing, with a foldable top made of some lightweight material. He had been cycling past the diplomat's house early one morning when he saw it and stopped to admire it.

Soon the Frenchman came out to walk his dog. They got talking and in about fifteen minutes they had settled on a price. That's how Mike functioned. Impulsive decisions, half of which turned out right, which was about the same for more carefully pondered decisions. The diplomat said he would get the papers transferred if Mike paid him five hundred more, which he did. Even so, Mike got it for a song. By the end of the week, the jeep was standing in Mike's driveway. But he hadn't been able to take it for a really long drive because of all the flying he was doing.

I applied for leave the next day and Nikki signed the chit. Shiv's university would anyway be shut for those five days. Mike said Jyoti was coming along as well. We knew they were getting married soon. There was no billing and cooing in public because Jyoti wouldn't have it but they did spend Tuesday night at my place. Shiv slept on the sofa in the drawing room.

At six on Wednesday morning we set off. Our destinations were wherever there were army guest houses. The Brigadier had seen to that. Shiv had an uncle in some government outfit that operated on the northern border so he too had chipped in with a guest house. Jyoti and I split the petrol bill. Food was dutch. I had briefly wondered if I should ask Nikki to come along but decided not to. Quite apart from the obvious reasons, there was nowhere in the jeep for her to sit.

We took turns at driving. Jyoti turned out to be a surprisingly good driver. By around three that afternoon we were at the bottom of the ridge outside Chandigarh that eventually creeps up into the mountains. The air was crisp and smelt of fresh pine and moist vegetation. The slopes were green after the monsoon. The sun was yellow and the sky was blue. Together they induced a sense of languor and longing that I had always found slightly distressing. I preferred early mornings and the darkness. Mike navigated us with an aviator's precision so we reached the first guest house at seven-thirty sharp. It was in the middle of a forest, in a compound belonging to the army.

That first day of our holiday set the pattern. Off by

nine after a heavy breakfast of eggs, parathas, potatoes and lassi, drive around aimlessly the whole day with Mike pointing the way, reach the next guest house by eight in the evening, drink till nine-thirty, eat and go to bed by eleven. Shiv grumbled a little about this but I must say I liked the predictability of the start and the end of the day. The days indistinguishably merged into each other.

None of us spoke very much during the trip. Each one enjoyed the trip in his or her way without trying to force it on the others. Nor did we do any traditional sightseeing. But we did stop when we came across some old church or temple. Shiv often came up with some history about them but I think for the most part he was just having us on. No one paid any attention.

One evening, while Shiv and Mike had gone off to the nearest town to buy beer, Jyoti asked me about Mala Auntie. We were sitting on the broad verandah where the river flowed alongside. The sun had been down for a while but the caretaker hadn't turned on the lights yet. It must have been the sense of anonymity that darkness sometimes induces which prompted her.

'She is very well-read,' I said. 'Highly intelligent. A gentle yet no-nonsense person.'

'Will we get along?'

'I don't see why not,' I said. 'She will not try to run Mike's life. You can be sure of that. Nor will she expect you to have a bath first thing in the morning, do the puja before you bring her the tea at six. Nor even massage her feet last thing at night.'

I then told her about our visits to Mike's house over the last dozen or more years, the sense of calm in their house, the quiet motherliness of Mala Auntie and the easy deference to her by the Brigadier.

'If I may say so, old thing, you are very like her, at least where Mike is concerned. Unobtrusive command and all that, you know, bossy without being crass about it.'

I couldn't see her face in the darkness. But I think she was quite taken aback. She didn't say anything. Instead she asked about Mike.

'Is he a mama's boy?'

Shiv and I had ribbed Mike about this countless times. Mike could not and would not disobey his mother. She hardly ever asked him to do or not do something. But if she did, then that was that.

'He is like a well-trained puppy and she is like an undemanding master,' I said. 'Don't have any concerns on that count. Mala Auntie will not come between the two of you.'

Then she asked if Mala Auntie would expect Mike and her to live at her home.

'I have a company flat, which I don't want to give up. It's a bit small but enough for us for the moment. Later we will see. Anyway, it is just a few kilometres away.'

Once again I assured her that Mala Auntie would not be in the way and told her that she was an extraordinary lady. Jyoti didn't say anything for a while. I suppose no amount of reassuring is of much use when it comes to this particular relationship. I wondered fleetingly if Mala Auntie would also ask me about Jyoti. I hoped not.

Jyoti started saying something just when the caretaker came to turn on the lights. She got up and said she was going for a walk. I waited for Shiv and Mike to return and thought about Gibbsy and his mother who lived in far-off Nagaland. As if that was not far enough, he was lucky in the way all Foreign Service officers were. They simply went away a few thousand miles. Then, when they were on home leave, everyone was on their best behaviour. There had been no word from the two of them but that was par for the course. Gibbsy and I didn't need to be in touch at all. We instinctively picked up the beat when we met.

Mike and Shiv came back presently, lugging not one, not two, not three but six cases of beer. Seventy-two bottles. We had only three days to go, which meant we had to consume six bottles per head per day.

'Before you say anything,' Mike said to Jyoti who had come back, 'one of the cases is for tips to the staff. They feel very good to be able to drink angrezi.'

It was, on the whole, a very nice trip. At eight on Sunday evening I was back home.

Madhavi was waiting on the verandah.

· · ·

It was past nine-thirty by the time she was ready to go out for dinner. She was in her usual haute couture attire: thick T-shirt, knee-length shorts, two-strap sandals, no make-up, no perfume, just a lot of cold cream or something which had a very agreeable smell. We walked down to the bigger of the two local markets and found a table at the Moti Mahal because Madhavi wanted 'Indian'.

After the beer had been served, as was usual in these days of prohibition in a large khullar, and she had gulped down half of it and after the very large order had been taken, she explained.

'I am back in India for three months because I persuaded them to pay me even if I wasn't there. If I live here with a dollar income, I will be able to save some and then pay for myself for the extra three months that I need there from January to March. And I am at your place because Sharada and Ashok are away till Wednesday. You don't mind putting me up for a couple of days, do you?'

'No, you are welcome. But I can book you into a room at my club. My treat in case you are short.'

'Let's decide that tomorrow, shall we? Right now, all I want is another beer, a full tum, and a clean bed.'

In the end, she stayed the whole week because she had got the dates of Sharada's return completely wrong. Sharada was coming back only on Saturday. She told me getting dates wrong was her forte. She had missed flights, movies, dates, deadlines and much more because of this.

'It's a thing in my brain, I think,' she said. 'I just forget.'

It was a strange experience on the whole. Although

she clearly preferred to stay at my place, she made no effort to spend time with me. We barely saw each other because she slept late and woke up only around lunchtime. Then she went out and came back after I had gone to sleep. I had to give her the spare key as a result.

I, for my part, even though I hardly saw her, felt content that she was there. Sometimes when I came back from office, I would find a second dish on the table. When I asked the maid about it, she said memsahib had made it. Twice, she stuffed the vases with flowers.

Often, two or three of my books would be lying open on the little side table near the sofa. Once or twice I had to put her pillow back on her bed. But I left the books where they were. The next day there would be a fresh bunch. The records would be strewn about on the table, too.

I felt like an inn-keeper. I had to make sure that there was enough food in the fridge, that her clothes went for a wash and got ironed, and that her room was cleaned daily. I was quite used to guests because every now and then some relative or other, not to mention my parents, would come to stay for varying lengths of time. But unlike Madhavi they were early risers and posed no problems at least where the servants were concerned.

One evening, I found her lying on the sofa, reading the latest Mills and Boon. I had a shelf full of them. Sunidhi used to hate them and berate me all the time. They were actually the six-pack samples which came every three months to the marketing people. The girls in the office shared them and eventually they would be dumped on me because I found them very enjoyable.

'I will be off tomorrow,' she said. 'Sharada will be back by about seven. It's a morning train.'

There was nothing much to be said to that.

She handed me a bottle of aftershave.

'I had got this for Ashok but never mind. I will get him one next time.'

A little later she suggested she take me out for dinner. So we drove to a roadside place near the Chinese embassy that served excellent kathi rolls. We went for a movie afterwards and the next morning, after breakfast, she was gone. I wondered what she'd say to her cousin but then realized that she didn't have to say anything. Only my servants knew she had been staying with me.

I felt a little resentful and ill-used. Yet, I also felt that it was a compliment of sorts, even if perhaps an impulsive one. She'd been no trouble at all except for the late waking. I supposed she had also felt a bit awkward and done her best to stay out of my way. I had tried once or twice to suggest to her that she could have dinner with me instead of eating out every evening. But she made some excuse or the other.

Mike and Shiv had both been around once and gone quietly away after I told them about her. They thought I needed this diversion. They didn't know about Nikki. My attempts to convince them that there was nothing to it had been unsuccessful. They were not the type who leered and cracked lewd jokes but the way they studiously avoided the topic was a dead giveaway.

I had been trying constantly to analyze how I felt about her. I found out only after she left.

I missed her and wondered what there was to miss.

• • •

Nikki phoned on Saturday morning to ask if I was free to meet her. She sounded tense and I said I would go over to her flat. I reached there around eleven. She let me in and got straight to the point.

'The MD wants me to sack you immediately. He said to give you six months' pay and ask you to stop coming to the office from Monday.'

She saw the look on my face and continued. 'Frampton complained to the Big Boss in London that you were being obstructive. So the Big Boss called the MD who called me. Will you resign or shall I have to sack you?'

'Can it not wait till Monday morning?'

She said it could. So I sat down on her rocking chair and lit a cigarette. I smoked the thing down to the butt before I could speak.

'Which would you prefer, considering the outcome is the same?'

She sat absolutely still for a long time. Her eyes were slightly moist and I hoped I would never find myself facing the same or similar dilemma.

'I'll tell you on Monday,' she said finally. 'Let me talk once again to the MD and find out a little more.'

This was typically Nikki. Always calm and ever the one to hold her nerve the longest. We left it at that. I was too jumpy to sit still and decided to go for a long drive. She asked if she could come too and so we drove all the way to Agra, which we reached around three. We had hardly spoken. The shock was too severe and the finality of the MD's instruction left little to be said. We had not eaten because neither of us felt up to it. I turned the car around without entering the city, and we got back to Delhi by about seven in the evening.

I dropped her off and she didn't ask me to come up. I wouldn't have gone if she had asked because for the last hour or so I had been thinking of going to see Madhavi to tell her about what had happened.

'Right, then, see you on Monday,' I said and drove off home and sat on the verandah, where I drank nearly half a bottle of whiskey and smoked a whole packet. Thanks to the alcohol and the empty stomach, I was feeling very sorry for myself. No sooner than I had got over Sunidhi, this had happened. I wasn't very worried about finding a job but publishing was a small industry and word would soon get around that I had been asked to go. In fact, Frampton would make sure that it did. I eventually fell asleep around three on the chair and woke up at dawn, stiff, thirsty, hungry, and very angry.

I tackled most of that day with a huge hangover. It was only by six and after a long walk that I returned to normal. First Nikki called and wanted to know how I was. Then Madhavi called and wanted to know where

I was. 'I called you twice yesterday and twice today.' She sounded concerned but also annoyed.

I told Nikki I was fine and Madhavi that I had been in the office to finish some pending work. I was dying to tell her what had happened but it would have to wait till after Monday. Then I called an acquaintance in another publishing house and asked him if his offer to join still stood. We arranged to meet for lunch the next day and feeling much better, I got down to planning both a holding operation and an exit strategy. It was, after all, only a job.

In the event, thanks to Nikki, neither was needed.

• • •

Just before I set off for office, Nikki called and told me to go to the MD's house.

'He says he is feeling unwell but has agreed to see us. Come a little early.'

She was waiting for me in the garden. I could tell that she was furious. I asked her why.

'It's got nothing to do with you,' she replied. 'I am angry because they can't just order us around anymore. I have decided to tell the MD that if he won't stand up for us, I will.'

'Which means what?'

She looked at her watch and decided that there was enough time to tell me a little story about her father who had been in the army. He had been serving in North Africa in 1942, she said. He was a mere lieutenant with two or three years of service. His CO was an Englishman, a major, about forty years old, who had reached the top of the pole. They were in a dugout somewhere near Tobruk. It was the middle of summer and there wasn't much relief from the heat, sand and the flies. Water was scarce as always and the hours of boredom, waiting for action in which you could get killed or maimed, had everyone snapping at each other.

One day, Nikki's father's batman, an old soldier with over thirty years in the service of the King, told the major that he could not have a shower that day as there just wasn't enough water. The major called her dad over then and asked him to charge the old man with insubordination in the line of duty. Her dad refused. A huge row ensued but her dad stood his ground.

'I am going to the MD with this little story,' Nikki said as she stood up and went to ring the doorbell.

The MD, a decent enough man, was still in his crumpled white kurta worn over huge flappy pajamas. He looked miserable. His cold, he said, had gotten worse over the weekend and now he thought he was running a fever. Nikki was not impressed. She got straight to her story. When she had finished, the MD asked her the question I had wanted to.

'What happened in the end?'

Nikki said nothing. She just stared at the MD. I was seeing a side of her which I would never have thought had existed. She looked so utterly cold and resolute that the MD finally got the point.

'Aah, I see. The major got in the way of some friendly fire. Where?'

'I don't know, Sir. But my father used to chuckle when he thought of the incident.'

'I see. So you want me also to shoot Frampton?'

He and Nikki went over the sequence of events while I watched and listened. The MD sounded shocked when he heard the value of the order. Then he turned to me asked if I had demanded a quid pro quo.

'Well, Sir, I hinted to him that he could let me have one of his authors for my list. The book is about India, after all.'

'Was that all?'

'Yes, Sir. Why?'

'Well, Frampton seems to have suggested to his Freddie that you were demanding what he called an "illegal gratification".'

I sat very still, absolutely astounded. This was such a lie. I could hardly believe what I was hearing. But Nikki became even angrier. She stood up, said in a very firm voice that she was resigning, and went out. I followed her. She was walking very quickly and was almost at the gate when I caught up with her. She held up her hand, winked, got into her car and swiftly drove off. I did the same but only after smoking a cigarette. I could see the MD who had come out on to the verandah. He couldn't see me through the heavy creeper on his fence. He was looking shocked and bewildered. I saw him send his servant out, possibly to look for us. So I quickly stubbed out the cigarette and drove off. As to Mr Bloody Frampton, our Tamil accountant would have to be pressed into the breach.

Nikki seemed perfectly normal when I knocked and went in. She was giggling into the phone and waved me to sit down. I heard her arrange to meet someone for dinner and a film and I felt a slight irrational stab of jealousy. I waited for almost five minutes before she put down the phone.

'Well, what did you think?' she asked.

'Will you really quit?'

'If he insists on sacking you, three people will leave. Me, Janaki and Ms Aiyar.'

Again, I waited almost a minute for her to explain and when she said nothing I asked her if she had told them about the friendly fire too.

'As I said, it is not about you. It's about decency and good behaviour. The English can be found very wanting in both from time to time.'

We went out to the balcony for a smoke where she told me that this was the last time London was going to have its cake and eat it too.

'The MD was on the phone before you came in. He said he would speak to them. If they wanted that order, you would not be asked to go. Otherwise no order from India.'

I went down to the accounts department and found my saviour. I explained what I wanted. He looked around and asked me to meet him after work in the café downstairs.

I went home that evening with an envelope full of copies of Freddie Winters' bills from his 'illegal gratifications' in India. I called Nikki and said she could sleep easy. She wanted to know why and I told her that I'd solved the problem. She wanted to know how and I changed the subject.

'Are you going to the MD?' she asked.

I said I'd meet her in the morning. Then I drove to the MD's house and found on him on the garden where he was getting his head massaged. He was surprised to see me and said very brusquely that he was busy. Feeling like Bertie Wooster mentioning Eulalie to Sir Roderick Spode, I told him that I knew about Freddie Winters' capers. That was the last we heard of my sacking.

Nikki didn't ask any more questions. We sent Frampton a small order and he went into a long sulk. Childishly, he refused to part with the author I wanted. We ended up importing fifteen hundred copies at ten pounds per copy. If he had let us publish it in India it would have cost no more than a pound per copy, and sold as many as three thousand copies. The author may have ended up with smaller royalties but she would have had the satisfaction of seeing multiple copies of her book in every important library.

As for me, I was back to square one.

• • •

The episode had some interesting consequences. Frampton was transferred to Lagos. Winters stopped coming to India. The MD started paying more attention to Indian books, instead of preening over the sale of British and American books. He asked me if I would be his special assistant but Nikki stopped me from becoming an accomplice. Ms Aiyar, Janaki and I became good friends, having lunch together often. The lie that Frampton had told about me rankled. I wanted to throttle the swine but he was 5,000 miles away in Lagos.

Over the following months Nikki and I drifted apart but we remained close friends. She was the one I always consulted first on anything important. We met outside the office at least once a month. She said her new friend was a civil servant, just divorced and, dear me, an author of sorts. I asked her what he wrote and she said plays. That was well beyond me and I lost interest.

No one else seemed to be having any problems in finding authors but I was still missing one. I knew I would eventually deliver but the waiting was beginning to irritate me. I began to wonder if after what had happened the effort was worth it. I thought it was unfair to demand so much from one editor and so little from some of the others. But I said nothing.

From what I had gathered from my father, it was exactly the same in the IAS: they sent the youngest to the districts and demanded the most from them while the older officers sat in the comfort of their offices in the state capital or some other big town in the state. The result was that the politicians prevailed.

My father had tried to change this system and, for his pains, been sent off to Delhi to argue with the central government. He had got nowhere in the end and eventually gave up trying to reform the system. The least experienced people continued to be in charge of the most important parts of governing India.

Word had got out of Frampton's perfidy and the loss of faith it caused had a peculiar effect on moods and morale. I was now a middling senior because there were three other editors who were junior to me. I should have felt more rooted. But I started feeling unsettled. I couldn't rid myself of the feeling that this was not going anywhere. The parent firm was in trouble because of the prolonged recession in the West. The prolonged inflation there was causing fewer books to be sold while costs were mounting. There was a sense of futility in the air.

Madhavi and I met at least thrice a week, sometimes more. The mutual attraction was noticed by everyone, including, most importantly, by Sharada. Once or twice when she was away, Madhavi spent the weekend at my flat. She got to know Mike, Jyoti and Shiv well. They assumed that we would get married as soon as she came back after her PhD. I truly enjoyed talking economics with her. It was very different from Sunidhi who was not at all interested in it and tended to talk down at me.

Mala Auntie's book was accepted by a new but already well-regarded publisher. They tried to diddle her on the royalty but I took care of that. She would get fifteen per cent of the list price and not ten per cent of the discounted price to wholesalers. She was all smiles. Books, she had once told me, were physical evidence that you had once existed not merely as a body but also a consciousness.

Mike and Jyoti got married and moved into her official flat a mile or so from mine. It had been a quiet affair, held in their house, because Mala Auntie had ruled that it would be vulgar to invite more than a hundred people when there was such a terrible drought in the country. The Brigadier made up for it by getting enough beer and whiskey from the army canteen to drown the lucky hundred who were invited. I got the feeling that Jyoti's parents would have preferred something a bit larger but Jyoti, not wanting to annoy her future mother-in-law, had stood firm. She also ruled, in a sign of things to come, that there would be no honeymoon. What a bunch of tough ladies, I thought, we all seemed to be choosing. I wondered briefly about how Gibbsy might be faring on that count.

Shiv's papers were published by us as a high-priced book and it got good reviews. He presented a copy to his tormentor in his department who, he said, told him to write a book, not be content with just small essays. It was good advice and he said he was going to take it. He seemed to have gotten over his anger at not getting the assistant editor's job. The journal would have to review his book, he said, and that was much better for networking than being a factotum.

He bought me a small music system for my birthday. Madhavi and I spent long hours listening to my records on it. At her father's insistence, she had been trained in classical music. I was an instinctive listener, she said, good at recognizing good music. Her pet theme was that most musicians could do only some pieces well but they did those so superlatively well that the rest of their performances were assumed to be just as good. That's how record companies made money, she grumbled.

Yet, there was a sense of discontent, a strange inclination to resist the passing of time. It was like the last few days in Jubilee Hall, the post-graduate men's residence in Delhi University. That had been seven years back and we had all felt what Churchill had described, in a different context, as the end of the beginning. Life would never be the same again and that sense made all of us stay away from each other, or at least see far less of each other than we had until the exams had ended.

Perhaps it had to do with the fact that in a few months the Seventies would end. They had been a tumultuous decade, from every point of view, personal, professional, national, and global. India was unrecognizable from the time the decade had started. It had created a new country by breaking up Pakistan at the very start of the Seventies. It had gone through a period of dictatorship comparable to any in the world. It had reaffirmed its future as a democracy. The Constitution had been restored to its former magnificence.

It had been through a major economic crisis when crude oil prices had quadrupled in a matter of months. It had enjoyed the fruits of the employment bonanza that quadrupling had created in the Middle East. It had taken one of the worst droughts in its stride. No one had died of starvation. It was now coping with one more drought, worse than the previous one, and another quadrupling of world oil prices despite the fact that there was no proper government in charge.

I had fallen in love and found a job within a few months of each other. The love thing had unravelled and the job was also unravelling. I had emerged a less nice person after the first and had no doubt at all that I would come out even worse after this job ended, whether because I resigned or because I was dismissed.

On the whole, though, there was more to celebrate than mope about and I should have felt elated. At times I did. But it was hard to shake off the feeling that some precious things had gone and were going forever. The snail was on the thorn and the lark was on the wing. Yet, all was not right with my world.

There was a sense of ending, rather than beginning.

8

'Should I quit publishing?'

Madhavi and I were sitting on the back verandah facing the lawn. It was a cool evening but not yet time for a drink. The sky was unusually clear for the time of the year and I could see the stars through the trees. Delhi, someone had once explained to me long ago, lies in a mild depression that starts in Lahore and goes up to Agra. This causes a phenomenon called inversion which traps the cold air between the ground and 1,000 feet in the sky. That, in turn, leads to a haze in the sky. It is only when the atmospheric pressure rises that clear skies happen in Delhi. I had no idea whether this was true. But it didn't matter that evening.

'And what will you do, instead?'

'I have no idea,' I replied. 'But this job is beginning to annoy me. You know, except when I take the first call after the manuscript arrives. After that it is just send, receive, forward in an endless succession. I am just a postman. It's all very mechanical and boring.'

'So isn't there something else you could do within publishing?'

'Just accounts, personnel and marketing which is

just a fancy word for selling to reluctant wholesalers, who care only about what they'll get out of it. The book itself is irrelevant to them.'

She didn't say anything. I knew her well enough by now to know what she was thinking—why ask if you have already decided.

'It's not as if I have made up my mind. I am merely wondering if I am hoping for too much from what is, in the end, a business like any other, you know, produce and sell at a profit.'

'Well, you have studied economics so you should be able to be much more clinical about it. You are working in a multi-product firm which is in a unique industry. Every book is different from every other book. It's not like producing thirty-six brands of cornflakes or fifty-two brands of hand-cream. Each book is different and has a person behind it, you know, not unlike those Chinese shoe shops where Mr Lee or Mr Xi handcrafts a shoe for each customer. The only difference is whereas Mr Lee or Mr Xi makes only one pair of shoes on order, with a book you take your chances on a thousand copies.'

I briefly wondered what Nikki, Janaki and Aruna would say if they heard this soulless description of all that they held sacred. No wonder they regarded the economics list as a necessary evil. It brought in the money but was an affliction in every other way.

'That's all very well. But now that I know all this the questions remains: should I carry on or quit?'

We both knew it was a rhetorical question, asked

as much to provoke as to get a sensible answer. The thing was, as the Brits say, I had no other trade. Publishing is what I could do because publishing is what I had learnt. So we went back and forth for a while without reaching any conclusion. It was one of those conversations where both sides were being difficult, both were aware of it, and yet went on irritating each other. It was a pointless conversation which could not be concluded sensibly then. But we continued because it was nice to be with each other even if both were being unnecessarily difficult.

We went on like this for close to two hours when Madhavi finally went off, saying she had promised to help Sharada with something. She gave me little hug before leaving. We agreed to meet soon.

It was only seven-thirty so I phoned Mike and Jyoti to see if they were home. It had been a few weeks since we met because Mike was away so much and Jyoti had been on some training programme. Making a fairly long detour, I bought some kebab rolls on the way, the soft crushed ones that Jyoti liked. Mike was more a chunky meats man, preferring burras and the like.

Within a couple of minutes of my reaching their home it became clear that they had been quarrelling. Mike waved me to drinks shelf and Jyoti pointed out to the sideboard where she kept the nuts. I took out some ice from the fridge, poured some whiskey into two tumblers and asked her what she wanted. She waggled her wrist to say anything was would do. So I made her a vodka and tonic and sat down. No one said anything for a while.

'I can go off, if you two want to continue the fight,' I said.

Jyoti looked annoyed and it was Mike who answered. 'She says I should move into the executive cadre. I don't want to.'

'Why, or why not?'

'I will have to sit for exams.'

'So?'

'I might fail.'

'That's true.'

'You know I am no good at exams. I would have to study so hard that it will mean less flying.'

'For how long?'

It was Jyoti who answered. 'Six months at the most.'

'What's the advantage,' I asked her.

'Mike will be thirty in a year or so. It makes sense to pass that exam now. Once he passes it, another option opens up for him. If later on he wants to stop flying or has to or wants to reduce the hours he is up there, he will not have to take the exam then.'

I looked at Mike. 'If you took the exam, how many hours of flying will have to give up?'

'Pretty nearly half,' he said.

'That sounds reasonable enough. Why the fuss?'

'I might fail.'

'You can sit for it again,' said Jyoti, which I realized was the mistake that had triggered the fight.

Sure enough, Mike snapped back that it would mean again halving flying for another six months. They started wrangling again. I filled their glasses and suggested we all go out for dinner. Both said the other would go because the rolls I had brought would do for them. In the end we tossed a coin. Jyoti won so we left Mike fiddling morosely with his glass, desperate for more.

Soon after marriage Jyoti had got him to promise that he would avoid the third drink. Mike was a man of his word so he spent his evenings in misery. He had rashly promised his mother he would not smoke and foolishly promised his wife that he would have no more than two drinks at a time. She had told him that they were getting strict with the weight thing and that he needed to be careful.

For a while, Shiv and I had found a way out for him. We would give him not 60 ml but 120 ml per drink. But Jyoti had soon guessed what was going on and that was the end of that little subterfuge. Sons who are obedient to their mothers usually become obedient husbands.

• • •

We went to a Lebanese-Indian restaurant that had opened recently in an upmarket shopping centre. Jyoti sat sullenly all the way and I let her be. She detested confrontations of even the most trivial sort. I still didn't know her well enough to figure out why. Was it because she always got what she wanted and hated to be crossed or was it just a character trait? There was time enough to ask her why she was pressuring Mike to take that wretched exam. From what little I had seen of her, there were probably excellent reasons. She worked in the office, not in the air, and picked up a great deal of gossip. Maybe she had heard something that she wanted to use to Mike's advantage.

We were shown to a table by the window overlooking a small park. The music was 1960s, the softer songs. The lighting was perfect and there was no smell of cooking. There weren't many people dining. It was past nine-thirty so maybe they had eaten and left. We ordered and sat back. Jyoti looked at me challengingly, or so I thought. But I held my tongue and talked instead about the future of English academic publishing in India.

'Indians despise Indians, and Indian academics despise Indian academics the most,' I said.

She let me babble on. I had noticed this about her when we had all gone on that trip. She rarely offered an opinion on anything. When she spoke, it was either to find out something or to direct someone to do something. A quiet, self-contained and very self-possessed person, she rarely felt the need to chat.

It was not till the waiter had cleared the cold soup bowls that she thawed.

'Why is Mike so afraid of exams?' she asked.

'He tends to do badly in them,' I replied. 'He can't write answers the way they want them to.'

'But this is not like one of these college essay type things. There's some elementary maths, some basic statistics and common sense, you know, logic for solving little puzzles.'

'Does he know that?'

'I have told him dozens of times but he is being

very piggish about it. Now he refuses to even discuss the subject and gets angry like this evening.'

'Why not let him be for another year or so?'

'Well, yes, I would have except that there is a problem with that. You know there's been talk of nationalization and once that happens the bureaucrats will change the rules for getting into the management cadre. Mike knows all this but says he only wants to fly. But I know he will get bored with it in a few years.'

I agreed with her assessment. He constantly needed new things to do and once he had got the hang of it, he wanted to move on. Flying was the only thing Mike had not got tired of in about six months. Be it cricket or tennis or debating or anything with a hint of competition in it, Mike would do well a few times and then get bored. He could have been number one in any of these things had he persisted but that would not have been Mike. As a result, he had never formally excelled in anything. Mala Auntie and the Brigadier used to chide him about it once in a while but could only watch helplessly as their son flitted about from one thing to another.

Later, over some excellent jasmine tea, she asked me if I would speak to him. I said I would have to see and drove her home. I didn't want to get involved in their domestic tiffs. If Mike wanted to avoid the exam, she would have to persuade him to take it. In any case, I thought, Mike would not make a good manager. Having got used to highly-trained pilots, he didn't have the patience to deal with the slowness of others. Even in college he had tended to be short with students who were slow to catch on. But then, on the other hand, he had never had to contend with anyone like Jyoti, that too as a wife. No, I thought, best to watch from a distance.

We stood for a while talking at their gate and Mike came out to join us. He asked me about the dinner, enquired if Jyoti had 'had a go at you as well' and hung about defiantly while I finished my cigarette. I drove off presently, wondering strongly if this marriage was going to become a problem for me. I had seen it happen to my sister when she had been forced to mediate between a warring couple. Often, the two would make up and start blaming my sister. She had eventually had to cut them off almost entirely. The couple had ended up going their separate ways after three years. My sister had resumed her separate friendships with them but tended to blame herself when she was feeling very maudlin about something.

I hoped Jyoti would not insist on having her way. It wouldn't go down well with Mike. But I also knew that if she insisted, he would do her bidding. If their marriage lasts, I thought, it would be interesting to see which one of them worked harder to keep it going. At the moment neither seemed the type who gave in. Or, which was more likely the case, didn't bear a grudge when forced to do something against his or her will. My bet was that Jyoti would have her way, if only because Mike wanted peace and quiet.

I wondered how Gibbsy was getting along with his

wife. And before I dropped off to sleep, I thanked my lucky stars for saving me from Sunidhi who, in many ways, was like Jyoti—insistent, and usually right in her judgement. During our last six months together we had mostly been at loggerheads. Don't smoke, don't drink, don't eat so much, don't drive so fast, don't read trash, and lastly, don't touch me all the time when we are alone. I could neither open my mouth nor keep it shut without annoying her.

It was love in its purest form, I suppose.

• • •

By mid-November I had become very restless. Diwali had come and gone. My parents had come visiting as they did each year and stayed for a week. My mother, observant as ever, asked me if I had had girls staying over. I said no and she didn't persist. But she knew, as they say, a version of the truth. My father, observant in his own way, asked me why I was so irritable. I thought about it for a while and told him about my third author problem. He replied that I should go and see a classmate of his, Jambukeseswaran Subramaniam, an economic historian.

I perked up when he mentioned the name. He was not a superstar in the way the profession rated superstars but he wasn't a complete dog either. Having retired from the IMF, he was at least an A- in the rating game. In any case, I didn't have much choice. He lived in Sundar Nagar and I arranged to meet him the following week.

He had said his house was on the main road facing

the zoo and that he lived on the first floor. He opened the door himself when I rang the bell. He was a tiny man, just over five feet. He led me quickly to the balcony from which we could see into the zoo even while seated. He rang a bell by his chair and a servant came out with a tray with two glasses, an ice bucket and a bottle of Vat 69. His wife came by and said she had met my father a couple of times.

'The last time was in 1960, I think. Jumbo here says they were great friends in school and college but their jobs took them in different directions.'

She chatted for a bit and presently she went off after reminding her husband that they had to leave at eight. I looked at my watch which said it was just past seven. Time for two drinks I thought, and maybe a manuscript as well if I got lucky.

Dr Jambukeseswaran Subramaniam, PhD, author of seven books, then began to speak. He had a surprisingly deep voice for such a small man and a very calm measured manner. He spoke with the authority that comes out of complete conviction.

'India,' he said, 'is governed by fools and thieves.' He then named some of them. 'No other country in the world combines the two as efficiently as we do. We have perfected the art of picking the dregs to run our country.'

There was nothing to be said to this so I waited for him to say why he thought so. He came to it after the servant had come and poured his second drink, an extra large one because, as he explained, they were going to a Gujarati's house for dinner. 'That Patel fellow's economics would improve if he has a drink.'

I realized that he was speaking about the industries minister, a man who was quite well regarded. I said so, only to be told that it was not Patel but the secretary in the ministry, Marathe, who was the brains.

'Marathe keeps good whiskey,' said Dr Subramaniam. 'You should try it sometime.' He saw the look on my face and said, 'Don't worry, I'll give you a chit. He is a good friend.'

It was around seven forty-five when he finally asked me what I wanted. I told him. He said he had a manuscript ready on the fiscal history of India.

'It's a damn shame,' he said, 'what these fellows have done.'

'But, Sir,' I said, 'everyone seems to think we have done quite well.'

He didn't reply. He went in and fetched a small sheaf of papers stapled in one corner.

'This is the introduction to my book,' he said. 'Read it tonight and call me tomorrow morning at nine.'

Mrs Subramaniam then came in as if on cue and we all left together. I stuffed the papers inside my shirt against my chest partly to keep out the cold wind.

Turning onto Cornwallis Road that joined Khan Market to Sundar Nagar, I wondered what to do. It was just past eight and even if I drove slowly I would be home in less than fifteen minutes. I decided to see if Nikhila was home but changed my mind as I drove past. I just didn't feel like it.

So I went home, got myself some more whiskey and settled down to read the chapter I had been given. The style came as a complete surprise. There wasn't a trace of the academic lugubriousness I had got used to. Nor was there any jargon.

Dr Subramaniam wrote, chattily, that since 1955 India had adopted a political approach that would lead it into certain fiscal disaster. The judgement was backed by logic and facts and it was crisp and final. The prescriptions of Keynes were not meant for implementing socialist policies. It was like mixing tea and coffee, he wrote, or vodka and gin.

The only unanswered question, right at the end, was the last sentence. 'That it will happen is certain; when it will happen is anyone's guess.'

For the first time in weeks I relaxed. If the rest of the chapters were as good, I thought, I was done, my elusive third author was at hand. When I called him the next morning, Dr Subramaniam agreed to give us the book but not immediately.

'Last night Patel asked me to help Marathe with something and I am going to have to postpone finalizing the draft at least by a year.'

I asked him if he would at least sign a contract but he said he didn't want to be bound down. I argued and even pleaded. But he was quite certain.

'Patience, young fellow,' he said and rang off.

It was what we used to call the classic KLPD.

• • •

Madhavi had gone off to Bangalore for a few days to see an aunt or some other old person. Before she went we had gone to see the Test match against the West Indies. The Ferozshah Kotla ground was a lovely little thing with open stands and lush green grass and I wanted Madhavi to see it.

But there was a problem. In keeping with Indian traditions, it had no bathrooms so the women who came there had a very hard time. The men, of course, relieved themselves wherever was convenient, including behind the sight screen at the Delhi Gate end. If the wind was wrong, it could get quite smelly in the fine-leg, third-man region at that end. Fortunately, unlike the grounds in Madras and Bombay which are almost on the seashore, in Delhi the wind just doesn't blow most of the time.

Even though I was a life member of the DDCA, and entitled to a pass that would admit two, I had bought two season tickets for the Pavilion stand. The pass guaranteed entry and a seat but you had to sit where you found a chair. The tickets gave me the seats I wanted, just above the sight screen and just below the home team box.

We drove on my bike to the ground and parked outside the *Indian Express* office. The bike would be safe there, unlike at the ground itself where anyone could steal it. We walked to the ground and were seated by nine. The match was to start at nine-thirty, which it did. India batted first and scored over five hundred runs; the West Indies scored less than two hundred when their turn came and had to follow on. Then on the fourth day the rain came and the match ended in a draw when it didn't let up till well into the fifth day. It was very frustrating but being with Madhavi had made up for it. She seemed quite content too.

'Draws,' I explained to Madhavi later over tea and cutlets at the United Coffee House, 'means no result. I think it happens only in Test match cricket where twenty-two guys go at each other for five full days and end up with neither side winning or losing. Usually ninety minutes is enough.'

Afterwards, as we were walking past Regal Cinema, Madhavi decided that she wanted to see the film running there because it had a huge star cast. Practically every major actor and actress was in it. It should have had long queues but we got tickets very easily.

It was the worst film I had ever seen, the usual good-guy versus bad-guy stuff. It became so very bad as it went on that we decided to leave when the interval finally came around. I dropped her off and went home to my usual drink and dinner, feeling most dissatisfied with the day. The match which we should have won had been drawn, the film had been terrible, Madhavi who should have been with me was at Sharada's place and even the whiskey was running very low. To cap it all, I found, there was no dinner. I had forgotten that the maid had taken the day off.

Feeling quite sorry for myself, I walked down to the new Nirula's that had opened up at the Priya Complex, ate a couple of hamburgers and hot dogs and walked back home. It was too cold by then to sit on the verandah. So I decided, on the spur of the moment, to go and see what Madhavi was up to. That also proved a fiasco. She had gone to sleep, said the servant who opened the door when I rang the bell.

• • •

The week began the next day in its usual lacklustre way. Of my old friends, only Mike still lived in Delhi but he was away most of the month flying and spent the rest of the time with his family. I saw very little of them. Mala Auntie called me over a couple of times to drive the Brigadier to the hospital for his checkups. Nikki had gone into a shell and the office had become, at least in my perception, lifeless. The question of continuing in publishing kept nagging me. I just didn't know what else to do and neither help nor advice was available. The thrill, as the man sang, had gone.

I talked to Ms Bose after swearing her to secrecy, not that it was needed. She was by nature discrete and never saw any point in office gossip. She asked me what I wanted from the rest of the thirty-odd years I would be working. I said something fatuous about wine, women and song.

'Then this is where you should be,' she said. 'The money is good, we employ a lot of young girls and when you peel the onion right down to its core, we have hardly any responsibilities. It's just the thing for a snob like you.'

We argued about that for a while and she ended the discussion saying she would change her view of me only after I stopped despising everyone else.

'Most people think you are insufferable, you know,' she said.

I thanked her and left. I did wonder for a few seconds though if she were right. Sunidhi also used to go on and on about it to me. I wondered how long it would take Madhavi to get there. Probably not very long.

I discussed my job problem at length with Mala Auntie who said everyone went through these phases. She told me how the Brigadier had come close to resigning when he had been passed over for promotion because the chief's wife's nephew had to be accommodated. She explained how in the end it didn't matter because the army made it up in the next round after the chief had retired. Take a long view, she said, and don't get disheartened.

These were wise words but I knew deep down that it wasn't just the Frampton episode that was troubling me. For about a year, I had been getting a fairly close glimpse of the strategic thinking in the company and it was veering towards using India as a production base for typesetting rather than as a profit centre for publishing. Wages in England had been spiralling up for years and many companies were shifting their typesetting to India where labour was available at a tenth of British wages. This trend suggested that books would become less important for the Indian operation. And that meant that the editorial department would become an unwanted appendage which would be allowed to shrivel. I was unwilling to be a part of this arrangement.

Yet, I was reluctant to leave. I had joined publishing

not only because I needed a job, any job, but also because it was the most respectable of private sector jobs. It allowed all of us to pretend that we were serving a larger public cause even though we knew in our heart of hearts that it was no less commercial than the vegetable oil industry.

We cheated the producer of the books, whom we called authors, and we cheated the buyers of books whom we called readers. The former we paid less than he or she deserved and the latter we charged nearly six times more than it took to produce the book. We corrupted librarians for orders. We paid bribes to receive payments. We under-invoiced exports and we over-invoiced imports. It was a business at the end of the day but one with a large fig-leaf of respectability.

The university presses pretended to be a cut above the rest but for the most part they had been turned into vanity presses. If you belonged to the university, your book would almost certainly get published; if not, you took your chances. They were also very slow with their selling. Books could sit unsold for years and no one cared because no one was asking any questions. This worked very well for me, though, because of the number of very old books I had been able to locate in these university presses for my father.

Another new development was the gradual commercialization of academic journals in the social sciences and humanities. These could cost a few thousand dollars a year in subscription purely because their owners, usually a university or an association of professionals, had pumped in to boost their reputations. To be cited after being published in these journals was to ensure promotion. So competition was keen and the whole thing worked, in a significant part, on a you-scratch-my-back-I-scratch-yours basis. The editorial boards of journals were self-perpetuating oligarchies with all their inherent flaws.

Yet another big con was the 'review'. The only people publishers were ever willing to be nice to were the literary page editors of newspapers. I had seen Nikki bill and coo to some of these fakes. When I asked her about it she said, 'I get paid by the company to do it.' This, despite the fact everyone knew that reviews didn't sell books; they helped brand the publisher and maybe, after a few books, the author.

I worried sometimes that perhaps I was being too cynical. But it is only when you get to see the entrails of the good and noble that you realize how skin-deep they all can be. Veneer was a necessary condition for success but thankfully, it wasn't a sufficient one. To sustain the myths, there had to be something, at least, that was worth the candle. For what remained of my career in publishing, I thought, perhaps I should focus on those few things. Like finding the elusive third star author for my mediocre economics list.

No one would be able to say then that I had quit because I had failed.

• • •

One afternoon I was sitting in my room staring dispiritedly out at the grey sky that Delhi gets in December. The greyness wasn't because of clouds, it was the haze. It accentuated the dust on the leaves and dirt on the roads. It made me long for darkness from dawn onwards. Most people think of Delhi as a green, leafy city which it is, except that for eight months in the year the leaves are dirty.

There was still an hour to go before closing time. I had no work left to do. All the letters had been written. The three manuscripts for review had been despatched. The proofs had been seen and packed for the printer to fetch. The gossip, such as it was these days, had been indulged in and apart from some repetitive moaning about politics, politicians and inflation, there was nothing much to it.

Worse, the weekend was looming. With Madhavi away on yet another trip, there was nothing to look forward to because Mike was busy with Jyoti and Shiv was turning into something of a bore who never stopped talking about some plot or the other. I had been very short with him once or twice and he hadn't been around to my place for a couple of months. Worst of all, I had almost run out of books to read and was nursing the one I had. It was by Kingsley Amis, his new one called *Jake's Thing*. It was funny but in that gloomy way Amis affected, especially when talking about women. I wondered if I was becoming like him, an alcoholic cynic with traces of misogyny.

With nothing absolutely to do but wait for five-thirty, I went out to the balcony for a smoke. I found Nikki there, and she was crying. I lit two cigarettes, gave her one and asked her stop it. She took a few deep drags before speaking.

'They are going to shut down this operation,' she said. 'Winters has delivered his parting kick. The MD says he submitted a report to the Board saying we hadn't made a profit in a decade and were unlikely to for the next ten years. He rubbished all of us, said the MD had been lax in keeping laggards on and that the sooner we called the whole thing off, the better it would be for the shareholders.'

'He is right, you know,' I said. 'How much time do we have?'

'Minimum three and maximum six months. There seems to be some law about shutting down. They have to wait till they get permission from someone in the government.' I knew about this law from a book that was on my list and I also knew it didn't apply to publishing. But I didn't tell her that. Instead I asked:

'So how is crying going to help?'

'You are a perfect bastard, you know,' she said in sudden fury. 'Go away now and leave me alone.'

We agreed a little later to have dinner together at her place. The boyfriend, she said, was away travelling somewhere. 'Don't get ideas,' she added. I hadn't yet told her about Madhavi and me, not that there was much to tell except for the mutual attraction and the main thing it led to.

I went down to my accountant friend and took him

for some coffee to the restaurant round the corner. He gave me the lie of the land. Then I went home, had a hot shower, changed into some soft clothes, got myself a drink and sat down to think. There was something wrong, it seemed to me. Even if everything that Winters had said was true, which it was not, all that was needed was a fresh sales push. The books were fine, really, and the libraries were buying them on a regular basis. The losses seemed large on a cumulative basis but were quite small annually, and certainly nothing that could not be made up.

The real problem seemed to lie with the six branches whose costs were apportioned to us on a proportional basis. But given the time they spent selling our books I thought the proportion was too high. If that proportion were to be reduced, I had asked the accountant, would it make a difference? He had said it would. He also told me that often the profit or loss that a division made in a company was a fiction created by the top management. He asked me why I was asking and I told him the reason. He looked shocked and we parted with me comforting him.

Nikki had recovered fully. She gave me my whiskey. She had started keeping the brand after our little adventure. Her bureaucrat boyfriend, she said, was a teetotaller. I told her what I had found out. She again asked how I knew and I again refused to tell her. But she guessed anyway. It wasn't that hard, when you came down to it. She quickly came to the point.

'Okay, so the losses can be fixed by some accounting jugglery. But why would the MD agree?'

'I don't know. He may or he may not. He isn't a bad sort, you know, who dislikes books.'

'Perhaps we should play on that remark by Winters that the MD botched it. He is bound to be annoyed with that.'

We knocked it around for a while and decided to go and see the MD the next day. Dinner, as was usual at Nikki's place, was delicately cooked. Afterwards, we sat for a long while on her balcony which could be closed with some glass contraption she had installed. She turned on the heater so that her feet would remain warm. I went over my dilemmas with her and she went over hers with me. Her boyfriend seemed to be losing his glitter somewhat.

'Classic civil servant,' she said. 'Knows everything and knows it all the best. And what he doesn't know about isn't worth bothering with.'

'I thought he was a playwright?'

'Yes, that he is. But he writes plays about the civil service, would you believe it? And they even perform them at that awful club of theirs.'

I looked at her face and saw that the end, so to speak, was nigh. Mr Bureaucrat-playwright was soon going to get his posting orders from Nikki. She saw me looking at her, and gave her head an ambivalent shake.

I got the message and left. Life, never simple, was about to become even more complicated.

• • •

'Are you trying to teach me how to do my job?'

The MD was in a rare rage. I had picked Nikki up and we had driven across to the MD's house. He was having breakfast on the sunny side of his verandah and had waved us to the rattan chairs which, he said, had been in his family for sixty years. His wife gave us some coffee and went off, leaving us to it. Nikki told the MD I had something to say to him which I did. He listened quietly enough but when he spoke it was in white fury.

'No, Sir. I am merely saying that there is a way of giving us another year instead of shutting us down in three months.'

'And may I merely say that you should mind your own business and not try to play with the big boys?'

'Of course, Sir, you can say whatever you like. But I would still request you to consider my idea. You know I am not asking for too much.'

We went back and forth like this for nearly a quarter of an hour. The MD eventually calmed down and said he would look into it but could not promise anything. Nikki, who had said nothing at all, stood up abruptly, thanked him and beckoned me to follow her out.

'Now what?' she asked when we were on our way.

'We have to do some rabble-rousing, stir things up, you know, rattle the cages, shake the bushes?'

'How do you mean?'

'I read in one of those silly management books I edited a couple of years ago that senior managements derive power by co-opting middle management like you. They let you into a secret that they know will cause trouble and expect you to play their game. The trick, said that guru, is to judge which secret is worth keeping and which one is not. I think this one is not.'

Nikki said nothing. She just looked out of the window. I could tell she was thinking hard, perhaps wondering if she was not ceding too much ground to me. When we reached the office, she went straight to her room instead of stopping by at her secretary's desk which is what she usually did. She told her secretary to stay put.

Since morning tea would be served in a while and everyone would be there, I thought I would mention the state of play then. But I had underestimated Nikki. She soon came out, clapped her hands for attention and asked everyone to gather around. Then she told them what was afoot. There was great indignation, some wild threats and the general confusion that greets unexpectedly nasty news.

I thought of the few times in school when class teachers had announced the cancellation of a trip or a picnic or a game. But people are like sheep and accept anything eventually. To get them to react, you need troublemakers, people who lie, cheat and incite.

Nikki assigned me that role. Over tea when there were only the seven of us present, she asked me to organize a signature campaign. The top sheet, she told me, would contain the paragraph that at once pleaded and threatened. The plea was to carry on; the threat was to chuck some fine sand into the works.

I went back to my room and drafted the paragraph

of open entreaty and veiled threat. Nikki cleared the fifth draft. I got it typed and, after lunch, I took it around for signatures. Once they saw Nikki's signature at the top, most people signed without looking. In about thirty minutes the job was done and I took the three pages to Nikki who asked me to take them across to the MD.

'And here, take this also,' she said giving me a copy of the office order making me the Keeper of the Proofs. 'Give it to him for his record.'

Madhavi was due back that evening. So I asked if I could take the rest of the day off. Nikki looked at her watch and said okay. I dropped off the two envelopes at the MD's office and went to the station. It was one of the new ones on the outskirts of the city. The railways had decided to terminate some trains there because the two old ones could not handle the traffic. The platform was clean, as were the tracks. There was a new railway canteen in the corner which looked very inviting. I bought some food and waited for the train to arrive.

Surprisingly, it was on time. In a rare demonstrative gesture, Madhavi threw her arms round my neck when she saw me and whispered a welcome suggestion in my ear.

And that's what we did before I dropped her home around nine.

• • •

Driving home afterwards, I decided to drop in on a friend who taught public policy in one of the colleges in Delhi University. It was an awkward time to turn up but now more than ever I was determined to get that third author. If they were going to shut us down it would be after I had managed to do what I had set out to do.

Varun, I thought, might have a few suggestions. He was always deeply involved in current affairs because of the courses he taught and knew a whole lot of academics, some of whom were pretty famous.

He wasn't home but his wife was. She was used to my unannounced visits and let me in, looking slightly annoyed. She asked me to look after their older kid, a boy of about seven, while she put the younger one to bed.

'Varun will be back in about fifteen minutes. He has gone to drop his sister home in Chit Park.'

I sat down on the sofa and waited. The boy asked me to tell him a story. I ignored him. After a while he wandered off somewhere and presently Varun came back. I opened the door for him and he grunted when he saw me.

'Drink?' he asked and without waiting got out some army rum and poured me half a glass. I filled it with water from the fridge and we both settled down with cigarettes.

I got straight to the point and told him about my problem. 'Find me some famous bugger to write a book. He doesn't actually have to and a simple contract signing will do.'

If Varun was surprised at the cynicism of the

suggestion he didn't show it. Instead he asked me to wait for his wife to come down.

'She has a relative who is famous but he is not an academic. So he meets half your requirement. That shouldn't matter because he is very well known indeed.'

He wouldn't tell me who it was and I had to wait for Sudha to come down which she managed to do after about twenty minutes. Varun told her what I wanted as we laid the table for dinner and she heated the food. When all of it was on the table and we had sat down, she said her uncle was just the man for me.

'He used to work in the government and has just retired. If you recall, he got into a major controversy over some banking thing. His name was in the papers for nearly two years.'

I said okay and after dinner she gave me his phone number and address, which was quite close to where I lived in one of the newly-built houses in Shanti Niketan. It wasn't quite the thing I was looking for but I saw no harm in paying the old boy a visit.

I phoned him the next day and he said to come over that evening. I rang his doorbell exactly at seven and a servant led me to a drawing room that was typically former civil service. I had grown up in them. It was full of ancient and very valuable furniture. This had become a pattern now. Spanking new houses filled with antique furniture. The bureaucrats who built their homes just before they retired usually exhausted almost all their money on the huge plots they bought and the construction cost. The size of the plot was directly proportional to the post from which they had retired. It was a stupid vanity but much of the civil services had become just that.

Without the money to buy new furniture, they moved in with the jumble they had collected over their careers. More often than not, the furniture was bought from the PWD which held sales from time to time. Not open sales, mind; just by word of mouth. You could get top class almirahs and sideboards and dining tables and side tables and all sorts of other things made of Burma teak or Thai rosewood for as little as fifty rupees.

The game went like this. Some well-meaning head of department at some point would say it was necessary to refurbish the office and that new furniture was needed for that. The file would go up and down and the financial sanction would come through after a couple of years. The old furniture was then hauled off to the PWD stores which, naturally, were so small that they soon started to bulge.

So to dispose of the excess they invited the sahibs to buy what they needed. It has to be said, though, that the whole thing was fully democratic and clerks competed with very senior secretaries to the Government of India. The scam was that some sahib, at some point in the distant past, had made the rule that such disposal could only be at book value because the government could not make profits from the sale of second-hand furniture. It was just one more racket the bureaucrats had devised for themselves but no one thought of it

210	*T.C.A. Srinivasa Raghavan*

as such. So after a quarter of a century, almost all of the old government furniture had moved into private hands and the government offices were filled with plastic, steel and cheap plywood. Perfect equilibrium.

My host, Mr Tukaram Sakharam Shrikant, came down after about fifteen minutes. This was the other thing: senior and retired civil servants always made you wait. It was just one more thing that went with their status. My father had once told me that the British never used to do this and that it was a very Indian thing, honed into a fine art after 1947. 'LBW. Let the bugger wait' was the civil service leitmotif. It was petty, rude and pointless. But there it was, and you could do nothing about it. My father drew the line at ten minutes.

Mr Shrikant, it turned out, knew my father and my uncle from the days when they had served in the old CP and Berar which was now a part of Maharashtra, created in 1956 along with a dozen other states on the basis of a common language. He enquired after them and I told him they were fine. He then asked me what I would have to drink and I said whiskey, Sir, please. Then he asked me why I had come and I told him.

He said he had just the book for me. It is almost ready, in fact, he said. While we were waiting for the bearer to get our refills, I asked him what it was about and he told me about it in great detail. Most of it was the story of his heroism in the face of political chicanery, double-dealing and corruption. But I could see that at its core, it was a bestseller, depending on how much he chose to reveal.

It was almost ten by the time he let me go. I was slightly drunk after four whiskeys and very hungry. But more than that, I was very satisfied. I now had a talking point which, if it could be converted into a contract, would be a big relief.

In the event, that did not happen. Mr Tukaram Sakharam Shrikant suffered a heart attack a few days later. My luck was playing truant again.

9

It was end January and I had yet to find the third author. The MD had summoned me one day soon after New Year's Day and told me that London thought I was 'no longer an asset to the company'. He said the Frampton affair and the Winters 'blackmail' had left them with no option. He made it clear that he wanted me gone immediately. I told him I would think about it. He knew I could not be sacked without notice, which meant I had at least three months even if I was asked to quit that very day. That meant I had till the end of March to find the third author as well as a new job.

I wasn't too worried either way. The problem was one of sequencing. If I found a new job first, then although I would not be under pressure to find the third star author, it would give me immense pleasure to add him or her to my new employer's stable; on the other hand, if I delayed finding another job, I might find myself without both—a new job and a new writer. In the end, I decided against finding a new job until I had found the elusive star. I could leave properly rather than with my tail between my legs because officially that is what they would say, that I'd fallen down on the job. So, starting that day, I had eighty-five days in which to redeem my reputation.

The days ticked slowly by. Madhavi was busy with her thesis and we met only a few times for a cup of tea. Mostly, we talked on the phone. We had developed a comfortable friendship without complications. Both of us were preoccupied. Neither made any demands on the other. She told me once that Sharada, in her usual old-fashioned way, had asked her the previous evening if we were 'in love'. She had said no but Sharada had not been convinced and told Madhavi to be careful because I was 'not her type', whatever that meant. We had had a good laugh but Sharada's question had opened up a third front for me, and a second one for Madhavi.

Physically, at least, my other friends had drifted away. Mike and Jyoti now spent a lot of time either at his home or hers or with their aviation friends. I preferred to meet them at his parents' house. I had options there which I didn't in other locations. I could talk to the Brigadier or to Mala Auntie. Mike and I remained close as ever. He dropped in just before dawn one Saturday on his way back home from a flight that he had just brought in from Paris, he said.

He stayed till noon, and we talked—he mostly about his problems and me too about his. I didn't tell him I had been put on notice. Nothing much seemed to have changed in the two months since we had last met. But I could see it was only a matter of time before he caved in and took the management cadre test. Jyoti had once told me that the difference between Mike and me was that while he sought always to please people I wanted others to please me.

In a moment of intense irritation she had said, 'When they don't, you just ignore them.' I said nothing. There was no point because I suddenly realized I didn't care what she thought. Mike was my friend and if I could please him, well, that was enough for me. He left just after noon saying he would sleep till Jyoti came home around seven. They had to go for a wedding reception after that. One of her relatives, he said.

Shiv had gone abroad on a post-doctoral fellowship to Australia. He came by the evening before he left to thank me for introducing him to Ms Bose, with whom he got on splendidly. Twelve of his sixteen papers had been accepted for publication and the book would be out in a few months. The Australian university which was hosting him had offered him a permanent position and he was wondering whether to take it.

Again, to him too, I said nothing more than to warn him that Australia was in the initial stages of civilization. He grumbled about how hard it was do research on his chosen field except in England. I was reminded of what a professor had said about another, that in the end, he would be cremated in Golders Green in London.

We shook hands when he left, the first time in our lives. We both knew it would be a long time before we met again. I was surprised to find that I would not miss him at all. Perhaps Madhavi was filling the space he filled now, of academic trivia, politics and heartburn.

I had of late taken to frequenting the bar at the club, where I went after office. It was a peaceful little place, tucked into the corner of a large garden. There was a verandah with a dozen chairs where one could while away a couple of hours doing nothing more than wondering if one should have a fourth whiskey or if three were enough. Once, when I had mentioned this to Madhavi she said I was lonely but didn't offer to do anything about it. I said I preferred my own company as I never said silly things. She got that a bit wrong and sulked for a bit. Her comment did set me thinking, though: why was I spending more on whiskey in a bar if could spend so much less at home?

I never managed to work that out because one day, while I was starting my bike to go home from the club, I severely damaged my knee while kicking the starter. Later, at the hospital, they said I had torn the cartilage. But that was after a few hours and a morphine injection to help with the pain. It was humiliating to have to lie there by the bike, hoping someone would come and help. Eventually an old couple delivered me to a nearby hospital and I spent the night on a bed in a corridor, drugged with morphine and shocked into a stupor over how quickly things could change. I asked the couple to call Mala Auntie but not until the next day instead of straightaway after they got home.

She came looking for me the next morning, took one look at me, grimaced, scolded me for not getting in touch last night, got me discharged and transported me in her car to the military hospital. Her driver more-

or-less carried me to the car, into it, out of it and on to the gurney.

The Brigadier was waiting there and he pulled some rank so that I was operated on immediately. It was nothing much. I came out of the general anaesthesia very thirsty. The nurse said I could not have any water for at least half an hour but when she went out, Mala Auntie gave me a cold 77. I gulped it down, gagged and retched. The Brigadier laughed and went off somewhere. At five pm they said I could go and I managed to hobble to the guest room in their house and fall into a deep sleep. I slept through till nine the next morning to find Madhavi chatting to Mala Auntie.

I said hello to them and she handed me a glass of water, from a safe distance. I gulped the water down but this time it didn't come bouncing back. Mala Auntie slipped out of the room quietly but Madhavi waited for a full five minutes before coming and sitting by my side on the bed. She squeezed my hand and said I was a fool not to use the car more. I promised her I would start doing that as soon as I was fully mobile again.

Presently she went off and I gradually got my bearings back. The doctor had said I should not walk for three days and even after that I should 'take it easy' for at least a fortnight. So of the eighty-four days I had reckoned on, fifteen were knocked out. I had already expended nine, so I was down to sixty days in which to find my redemption. Thanks to the aftereffects of the anaesthesia I must have drifted off to sleep. I woke up with an intense throbbing pain in my knee but had no idea what to do other than just wait for someone to turn up.

It was almost an hour later that Mala Auntie came in with a tray of lunch. I asked her for a painkiller and slowly the pain came down. The relief was so great that I found myself telling her my sob story. She heard me out without a single interruption and left saying she had to see to lunch for the others but that we would talk later in the evening.

I slept off again and woke to find Mike and Jyoti looking down at me. They pulled up a couple of chairs and sat down and said they were going to be there for the next few days. 'Mummy's summons,' said Mike. 'Bedpan and the like.'

I realized then that I hadn't been to the bathroom the whole day and the two of them helped me to it. It was frustrating and humiliating but there was nothing to be done. Jyoti left the room for a while and returned a little later with a tray, a decanter, water, ice and four glasses. The Brigadier and Mala Auntie joined us soon and we all drank a lot whiskey. What else was there to do anyway?

Around nine or so, my dinner arrived and everyone left after watching me eat. Mala Auntie, on her way out, while handing me my medication told me in a very soft voice not to worry about finding an author and so on. There was a fleeting twinkle in her eyes which I wondered about briefly before falling into deep sleep.

As on the previous day I woke to find Madhavi on the chair by the door. I said hello and asked her to call

Mike. She asked why and I pointed to the bathroom door. She said it was not yet seven and everyone was asleep. She had been let in by the cook who was just starting to brew the morning tea. Then she came over, pushed me up and helped me to the bathroom. I was wearing only a long kurta and if she saw anything, she didn't flinch. When I returned to the room, she poured me some tea and said she had sneaked out, telling Sharada that she was going for a walk. We talked about this and that, my knee, her thesis, my problems in the office, her money situation, my plans after March and hers as well.

'She asked again last night about you,' she said. 'She was very direct and wanted to know if we were 'serious'. I ignored it but I know she will return to it.' I wondered whether it was Sharada who wanted to know or Madhavi and after a while asked her that.

'I am engaged to someone in the US,' she said. 'But I haven't told anyone yet.'

• • •

My knee slowly recovered over the next few days. Mike took me for a review to the hospital where they took off the brace and the bandage and placed a knee support over it. I was asked to wear it for two months and told not to start my bike. I had anyway decided to sell it.

It was time for me to go home, which I did very early the next morning. I had been away for eight days and the place was quite dirty. I dusted one of the cane chairs on the verandah, lit a cigarette, and sat down to wait for the maid. I thought once again about what Madhavi had said the last time she had seen me. I should have been very disappointed but for some reason wasn't. Maybe I would have been if we had become more intimate but she hadn't let that happen.

I wondered if it was from a sense of loyalty to the chap she was engaged to or just that I wasn't inviting enough. That odd week that she had spent at my place now made some sense. I had never had girls stay over before and sleep in the guest room. On the whole, I decided, it was just as well because I still wasn't ready to get into any permanent arrangements. Neither girls nor money were in short supply which they would be if I went the Mike and Gibbsy way.

The maid came and I sent her off to buy some milk, bread and eggs. She came back and made some breakfast and after she had cleaned the house and gone I hobbled over to the bathroom, had a shave and shower and got into bed and, exhausted after the morning's effort, dropped off to sleep. I woke up because the doorbell was ringing.

My bedroom door also opened on to the verandah and I found Madhavi standing there, looking very pretty in a pair of olive green shorts and white T-shirt. Her skin and hair were glowing and her eyes lit up when she saw me. She rushed into my arms, forgetting that I was still very unsteady on my feet and almost knocked me over. She helped me into the bed, pulled up a chair and sat down.

'Coffee or tea?' I asked her.

'Nothing. Just listen,' she said.

She said, very calmly and without ado or fuss, that she had phoned her fiancé in the US and they had talked for a long time, which cost an arm and a leg. In the end, they had both agreed that it wouldn't work. I didn't ask any questions, just listened quietly wondering if that was why she was looking so happy.

'After that,' she said, 'I called my thesis supervisor to ask if the revised thing was okay and he said it was. It's done, man, done, over, finished, I can submit now. You are the first person I am telling, not even Sharada or my parents.'

I congratulated her, finally comprehending why she was looking so buoyant. There was a new lightness in her manner, something I had not seen so far. She talked continuously, hopping from subject to subject and I mostly listened. Around one o'clock she went off to get some lunch from the Chinese restaurant. Then she fetched some gin and tonic from the dining room and we had a couple of very long drinks each. We then ate out of the cardboard boxes and soon I started feeling drowsy.

I lay back on the bed and must have dropped off because when I awoke she had gone, leaving a note that she would be back soon. And sure enough she came back in about half an hour. It was five in the evening and I realized she had spent the entire day with me. Again she talked, and I listened and felt complete in a way that I had never felt before, not even with Sunidhi, not even on that strange night in London when despite the breathlessness having gone, and after all that bitterness, we had settled down like an old married couple. This was a different feeling, of quietness and calm and well-being that I didn't remember ever experiencing anywhere outside of my parents' home.

It was, what can I say, quite wonderful.

We had dinner together, this time with some of the whiskey that Mike had given me. Exactly at ten, she patted me on the head and said she would have to go which she did shortly, taking my car with her. The last but one thought in my head as I fell into a deep sleep was that I was still short of that damned third author. The last thought was that Mala Auntie had asked me not to worry.

Two women, reassuring me in their own confident ways, and in equal measure.

I stayed home for another week, and Madhavi, not having anything to do now I suppose, came every morning and stayed till night. It became a firm routine, the eleven in the morning to ten at night thing. On the fifth day of this, which was a Friday, she drove me to the doctor because Mike was off flying somewhere. We picked Mala Auntie up because she had the hospital card. The doctor said I was fine now but not to strain the leg for a few weeks more.

We went to the club from the hospital, had some beer and lunch. Mala Auntie brought me up to scratch on the news, which was mostly about Mike and Jyoti. She tried hard to hide her dislike of Jyoti but succeeded only in convincing me that she would never stop resenting the woman who had, in a manner of speaking, taken her only son away. Madhavi listened attentively, which was surprising because she barely knew that family. Afterwards, we dropped off Mala Auntie who told me to come for breakfast on Monday because she wanted me to meet someone.

• • •

The weekend passed uneventfully. Madhavi had gone off somewhere with some friends and I read a few books in bits and pieces. I noticed how they were getting longer and wondered why. I had a shelf full of late-nineteenth-century volumes that had belonged to my father's father. They were all around a hundred and twenty-five to a hundred and fifty pages long in the pocket book size whereas now the number of pages had pretty much doubled, that too in the larger size that was now standard for books. I made a mental note to find out how and why this had happened. Ms Bose would have some idea, I thought.

On Monday morning I called the taxi from the stand near Malai Mandir and went for breakfast to Mala Auntie's house. I found her sitting on the verandah with a balding white man with a goatee. She introduced him to me or me to him, I am never quite sure which is which. I recognized the name at once. William Moon had been a leading India expert for the last twenty years, ever since he had come over in the mid-1950s to study the economy. He had since written extensively about it and had now reached the stage where unless he certified something as being okay, it remained just a shade below par. He looked very old but Mala Auntie told me they had been contemporaries in Cambridge.

'Bill has written another book,' she said. 'About the economy.' The penny finally dropped and over a long and leisurely breakfast, Dr Moon agreed to let me have the manuscript. In the end, it turned out to be as simple as that.

It reminded me, for no reason that I could find, of the time when as a thirteen-year-old I had developed an abscess in my tooth. The pain was intense but since it was late evening, there was no dentist to go to at that time. I had spent the night in agony. The next morning my father and I were at the dentist's clinic on Parliament Street at eight to be the first in line. The doctor took one look at my face, and gave me a shot of something that took away the pain within seconds and said the tooth would have to be pulled out. Physical pain was immediately replaced by mental terror which was every bit just as intense. In the end, though, it had been simple.

The doctor had pressed a chloroform pad on my nose, asked me to count till ten and I had passed out at seven. When I came to the tooth was gone, I was walking to the car with a heavy cotton wad in my mouth and hearing the wonderful words from the doctor who had come out to see us off, 'Sir, give him only ice cream to eat for the next twenty-four hours.'

Thanks to Mala Auntie, this too had been as simple as that with as wonderful an ending. My main problem at the office was over and I, for the first time in my life, touched her feet in the Punjabi style, to say thank you. She patted my head and murmured the usual benedictions and I went off to the office to strut a bit.

10

There's a certain light-heartedness that accompanies the unexpected solving of an intractable and stressful problem. I hadn't realized till now just how much the elusive third author had been troubling me. The failure to find one had portended a severe dent in my self-image and that had been bothering me more than I had known. So when one appeared out of the blue, and even though it was no thanks to me, the effect was immediately euphoric and as it would turn out, ironic.

I reached just in time for the morning tea in Nikki's room. Everyone was there. I sat down listening to the chit-chat and sipped my tea, which tasted unusually good.

Eventually, Nikki looked at me and asked why I was looking so pleased with myself. We argued for a bit over what such a visage might look like. Then, finally, I told them that I had decided to resign because I had found the third author, of impeccable academic credentials, and moreover a solid marketing bet.

'I come to go out with a bang, not with a sorry whimper,' I said, and immediately felt like an idiot.

Then I told them his name and they all congratulated

me because everyone had heard of Dr Moon. Nikki asked how I had done it and I said, in my silly mood, that I moved in mysterious ways, etc. I knew I was behaving like an ass but I was on a real high. I had suddenly realized that day, in that room, at that moment, how small the publishing world was. I could not wait to get out, though to what, I had no idea. It was not as if I was qualified to do very much else or that jobs were waiting to be taken. But the urge to escape was inexplicably strong. And I was determined to jump out of the window.

I looked at Nikki and saw a fussy woman who was stuck in a professional cul-de-sac. I looked at Ms Bose and saw a wonderful old lady who had come to terms with her lot in life. I looked at the rest of them and sensed disappointment in each of them, that they really hadn't thought that life would turn out quite this way. I knew I was being unfair. I knew I was probably wrong.

But I also knew that I suddenly wanted, with a desperation that I had not felt before, to get out. The old complacency about the job, when I thought it was ideal for me, had gone. Mala Auntie, who intended to help me keep my job, had had the opposite effect. I wondered what she would say when I told her I was getting out. Like me, she also thought that publishing was perfectly compatible with my temperament.

But what could I do if my temperament had changed?

• • •

Word got out in a jiffy and within a minute of my going back to my room, Mrs Singhal came in and asked me if what she had heard was correct. I said yes and her response took me by complete surprise.

'Beta,' she said, 'don't act in haste.' Then realizing how she had addressed me she became more formal. 'Sir, you hold this place together and if you go, it will start to come apart.'

I asked her to sit down and ordered some tea. I told her exactly how I felt about staying on and she listened carefully. We drank our tea and I asked her if she would take down my resignation letter. She fetched her dictation pad and I said whatever I thought was necessary. She prompted me from time to time to mention this person or that or to thank someone whose help I had not even been aware of.

We finished after about half an hour and she came back a little later with the typed letter. I signed the three copies which she took away silently, and that was that. I had put five years behind me in a matter of five hours, from breakfast at eight to lunch at one. The euphoria had subsided and now I just felt calm. No regrets, no apprehension as to what the future might hold, only the sense that I was not making a mistake.

Ms Bose stuck her head through the door and asked me to join her for lunch. We went down to the restaurant on the ground floor and after we had ordered she asked me to explain. So I told her.

'Wise decision,' she said. 'There's really not much hope for this cottage industry. But what are you going to do?

'I haven't thought about it. I decided only a few hours ago.'

'You know, when you first came here, when was it, five years ago I suppose, you were awful. Arrogant and dismissive. I remember how you used to be so scornful of my list. I was certain you would leave within six months as the others had done. But you turned out okay, I must say,' she said. 'I will miss you.'

I didn't know what to say and just looked at her. She gave me a short lecture on the way things were going in her areas. 'Slowly, the integrity is going. Too many academics now want grants and are willing to sing the tune the piper wants sung.' She explained how the government, for the sake of one political party, was gradually suborning the social sciences and how dissenting views were rejected.

'That uncouth boy you brought along, Shiv, he got out just in time. He would have been utterly miserable here.'

I suddenly recalled my promise to Kamini and her book on the Constitution and gave Ms Bose the gist of it. Her response took me completely by surprise. She suddenly became very animated and like Kamini in Madras six months back, she gave me a short lecture.

'The Constitution? Ha! Have you forgotten what that woman did with it,' she asked.

The woman in question was The Woman, Indira Gandhi, who had used the provisions of the Constitution to turn India overnight into a dictatorship from a democracy.

'It is tailor-made for just that sort of thing,' Ms Bose said. 'We simply copied the 1935 Act and you know what, young man? That thing was designed to ensure the supremacy of the central government. Our Founding Fathers failed to change an important aspect, of prior permission from the central government which formed the backbone of the British governance principle.'

I looked at my watch and saw we still had a few minutes to go before lunchtime ended. I didn't want to cut her short so I asked her how this had come about and she grew very angry.

'When the Victorian priests began to arrive here in large numbers in the 1870s,' she said, 'they found the "native Hindoo and Mohammedan" practices abominable and the people "shifty, untrustworthy and generally dishonest". They also had huge influence on the rulers, and persuaded them to frame laws—many of which persist to date—based on the overall principle that almost everything required permission from some designated authority at different tiers of the government.

'And you know what? This is the exact opposite of the practice in Britain where citizens can do anything that is not specifically forbidden by law. In India, they stood this on its head: citizens can only do those things that are specifically permitted. The Constitution reflects that underlying principle.'

I silently congratulated myself for having remembered to mention Kamini's pet peeve. It was Ms Bose's too and now nothing could stop it from being published by us.

I paid the bill and we went back up. I didn't see

much of her after that although we did manage to go down for long lunches twice more. On one of those she told me about herself, perhaps a bit more than she thought she would, and certainly a lot more than I wanted to know. It wasn't an extraordinary story or anything, no tragedies, no great achievements, nothing like that. It was just the sheer ordinariness that comprises the lives of most people, bland and good for the most part, that depressed me. School, college, a doctorate from Jadavpur, the choice between academics and a corporate life and finally a compromise: publishing. Like it did for most of us, the books business catered to the need for money and respectability simultaneously.

I asked her why she spoke so little and her reply has stayed with me. 'There's no point,' she said. 'People usually don't listen even when they have sought your opinion. It's best to say nothing or grunt.'

She gave one of her rare smiles and said, 'You, of all persons in this office, should know about that so-called law of yours, what you call the "law" of diminishing returns.'

I knew exactly what she meant because I also detested people who spoke for no reason at all. The thing was, most people did and my response had developed into ignoring them, which came across as arrogance and indifference. Most people expressed opinions without facts or facts without any context. It was very tedious.

I asked her why she had not got married. She said she had but that it hadn't lasted long.

'If you ask me why, I still won't be able to tell you why it didn't work. We got very bored with each other. One day, at exactly the same moment, we both voiced the same idea, divorce. When we were in love in the beginning we would have marvelled at how alike we were and seen that as an omen. Now it just seemed like the most practical solution. So we talked it over and decided to go our different ways. It seemed like far too much trouble to make all those adjustments and pretend and so on.'

She told me she had been single for almost twenty-seven years now. 'And, since you are wondering, no, there have been enough men in my life.' She told me about some of them. 'Nice enough,' she said, 'but you know, as you get older, you don't like to wake up to someone else's bad breath.'

I was wondering all along why she was telling me so much about herself and it was only later that I realized that she was certain she wouldn't be seeing very much of me anymore. It made no difference to her what I knew about her because I was unlikely to meet anyone who would be interested in her. In a way, I found it wonderful.

She asked me to stay in touch and that was more-or-less the last I saw of her because sometime towards the middle of my notice period she went off on her annual leave to England.

• • •

Around five that day, Nikki sent her secretary to call me to her room. I found her looking grim and determined and also, strangely, a little vulnerable. For a few moments she said nothing and just stared at me. I knew she was trying not to use expletives but in the end she was unable to.

'Bastard,' she said, 'you are an absolute motherfucker. Why the fuck did you not warn me beforehand? Why did you have to make such a show of it?'

She went on like that for a couple of minutes more and once again I just listened. There really was nothing much to be said because I knew that she knew that I had done the only thing left to me. She was angry not because I had resigned but because I had not discussed it with her.

Finally she cooled down and said, 'It's up to me to accept your resignation or not or from whichever date I choose. I am going to accept it but not before you have found yourself another job.'

'Well, actually, you know, I was planning to take a few months off and not do anything. So I don't really intend to look for another job for several months. What you are intending makes no sense. Let me go after the notice period, which is three months anyway. I promise you I will not leave any loose ends.'

She flared up again. 'It's not the loose ends that are bothering me, you fool. I need you here to see us through the next twelve months.'

I reminded her that the company didn't think so. She replied that she would sort it out with the MD. I told her he could go to hell and that I wasn't staying after the ninety days were over and that there was nothing she could do about it. We went back and forth like this for some more time and, in the end, she relented and said, 'Okay, on one condition. Find me a replacement.'

I thought that was reasonable and promised to try my best. I already had a candidate in mind, Madhavi, but if she declined, there were a couple of others that I could ask. Ours was a good name to work for, especially the economics list, and I was sure I would not have any difficulty in finding her my replacement.

I went back to my room and found some of the editing staff waiting for me. They asked the same questions, I gave them the same replies and presently they all went off home satisfied in the way people are to get it straight from the horse's mouth.

Just before I turned out the light, Nikki came and told me to come for dinner at her home that evening. 'I want you to meet someone,' she said and left before I could respond.

Driving home I wondered if I should go or not and decided it would be churlish not to. I went home, pottered about for a while with a sense of the anti-climax that comes when a high ends. I phoned my father and told him what I had decided and he sounded irritated. When he heard the full story he said I had done the right thing and put the phone down. I showered and drove to Nikki's place. There was a wedding procession going down the road where she lived and it was almost twenty minutes before I climbed the stairs to her floor.

I rang the bell, she let me in and I found two other

people already there, a man and woman whom I had never seen before. She introduced us. The man was called Ranji and the woman Jhanavi. He was a Tamil, she a Bengali. He taught economics at a minor university in England and she was a playwright and director of plays, she said. He seemed to be in his late thirties and she a little older. He had a deep voice which reminded me of Amitabh Bachchan.

Nikki asked me to help myself to a drink and the three of them sat silently looking at me while I poured it. Then after I sat down, the three of them stared at me and I felt as if they were going to interview me. I looked at Nikki and raised my eyebrows and suddenly, as if on cue, all of them started speaking at once. It took a while for them to sort themselves out and eventually it was Nikki who won.

'... are going to need your help.'

Slowly the story emerged. Ranji had written a book that he wanted us to see and Jhanavi had written a play she wanted to stage. I heard them out as they finished describing their respective works and looked at Nikki, completely mystified as to why she had roped me into this. She refused to meet my eyes and the evening dragged on. I made some desultory small talk and drank lots of whiskey and smoked almost continuously.

Nikki served dinner at about ten. When I went to help her with the plates, she gave me a quick hug and said, 'Sorry about this. I couldn't have got through the evening if you hadn't come. They are friends from college, you know, the earnest types. But they were nice to me when I visited them. Just another hour or so and you can go home after that if you want to.'

I shrugged and said it was okay and we all sat down for dinner. As usual it was delicious. Ranji seemed a nice enough fellow and even Jhanavi, who had a way of saying things that sounded disdainful of others, managed to keep it down. They left at about eleven-thirty in a taxi Nikki had phoned for. I turned to go to my car when Nikki asked me if I would like to stay for a bit and talk.

So we went back up and she poured me some whiskey and got herself some coffee. She kicked off her sandals, tucked her feet under her on the sofa. I lit two cigarettes and gave one to her and sat back, wondering what it was that could not have waited till the morning. I was in no hurry to go home and waited patiently for her to begin, which she did after nearly five minutes of total silence in the room.

'The MD wants me to resign,' she said finally.

I said nothing and waited for her to continue which she did after another long pause.

'They have finally decided to shut the programme down. He said if I resigned it would give them a good reason. It seems they have been wondering how best to go about it and someone in London suggested this way out.'

'I don't see the connection,' I said. 'How would your resigning help?'

'The plan is to wait for three months, go through the motions of looking for a successor and then say that they can't find anyone. Then they will bring in a guy from London to wind things up.'

'And what does this have to do with me?'

She looked at my empty glass and asked me to get myself another drink if I wanted one. I splashed too much soda into the glass and slurped some of it off before returning to my chair. I lit two more cigarettes and waited for her to resume.

'If you leave in March, there is no hope at all. With you around, and with Ms Bose propping us up, I could persuade them to give us some more time.'

I told her my mind was made up and that I was going. If they had decided to close us down a few more months would not be enough to change it.

'The real question,' I told her, 'is whether we can break even in twelve months and you know very well that we can't. There are too many structural reasons why that is impossible. So it is best to bugger off while they will still make a generous settlement.'

She said she didn't want everyone to think that it was because of her. I said people would think what they wanted to. She said it was terrible that the closure happened on her watch. I said it would not be her watch if she resigned six months before. I drank some more, and she started sipping from my glass. I hated anyone to do that and got her a fresh glass.

We batted like that back and forth for another forty-five minutes, our increasingly woozy minds no longer on the future but on the present, the next few hours. It was almost two when she said I could, if I wanted to, stay the night. I thanked her and said no and drove back home, perhaps a little unsteadily.

• • •

The next morning I woke up very thirsty and with a headache, a sure sign that the whiskey she had served was not what the label on the bottle said. I drank some water from the fridge. I showered and changed and made it just in time for the morning tea ceremony, or just a few minutes late.

Everyone was gathered around the fireplace, as it were, looking glum and worried. It was apparent that Nikki had given them the news. Aruna glared at me, whether for being late or for being instrumental in hastening our demise, I could not tell. Ms Bose merely nodded, too seasoned by now to be fazed by such things. The others looked down, away, out of the window, bothered only by what the future held or did not.

It wasn't easy to find jobs in publishing and we all knew that some of us would have a hard time finding anything at all. Age, competence, reputation, all would play a role and if I had to take a bet, I would say more than half the people in that room would be jobless even a year after losing their current one, or would be doing something that they didn't ever think they would be doing. It was like that in government and the public sector also where, even though no one lost their jobs, they did end up doing things that they had never thought they would.

One of my relatives in the Indian Administrative

Service, the premier government job, had spent the last seven years of his career supervising the animal husbandry department. He had a PhD in economics from a good American university and had entertained thoughts of being the finance secretary of the country one day. But he had fallen foul of the chief minister over some trivial thing and that had been that. Career over.

The huddle lasted till lunch. No one wanted to go back to their rooms. No one wanted to say anything very much, either. So we just sat around talking desultorily about this and that, as people do when someone dies. I had seen this when one of my friends in college had lost his father. I suppose finality of any sort has that effect. I had seen it when I had lost a semi-final table tennis match in a college tournament. I lost in the final point which could have gone either way. I remember just standing there for a long time, staring at the ball which had plopped down on my side of the net after hitting it, when it could just as well have dropped down on the other side.

I excused myself a couple of times to go out for a smoke. The editing staff was also gathered in groups of two and three. Strangely, none of them looked very concerned. It occurred to me as I smoked on the balcony that their skills were more saleable than ours because they were tangible skills while ours were based more on judgement and gut instinct. On my second foray out, two of them joined me and asked, as they might a doctor, how much time they had left. I told them at least six months, perhaps a year. They looked relieved because that was more than enough time to get new jobs.

I decided to go out for lunch and then to the university to spend some time with my economist friends. I went in to tell Nikki where I was going and that I wouldn't be back when Ms Bose asked me if she could come along. I didn't particularly want to take her but I could hardly refuse.

We went to my club and over a beer she told me that for some time now London had been asking her to join the London office if they did go ahead and shut us down. She said she would accept their offer. I congratulated her and more out of politeness rather than any genuine curiosity, asked her for details.

'You know,' she said, 'that's the trouble with you. You don't pay attention to others and their lists. Had you bothered to look at those quarterly reports they send out about export sales you would have seen how many of my books they buy over there.'

I asked her why and she came up with an explanation that should have struck me long back.

'Your books are about the Indian economy which no one gives a damn about. Mine are about things like democracy, society, law and so on which have a much wider appeal. The market for them here is very limited so you all treat my list with contempt.'

I don't know if it was the beer or the shock of that morning but she was getting positively belligerent now. She grumbled on for a while and I just sat and listened. She told me about her books, her authors, her copy editors, the fools in marketing, her English counterparts, her tussles with Nikki and just about everything else regarding her career and professional life. It was, I must admit, quite a tale, in which she emerged like a female Casablanca. I wondered if the other editors felt similarly. I knew I did.

'You know,' she said at one point, 'you are quite a sharp fellow. Do you remember that day when we were smoking on the balcony, talking about how it was random small events that changed the course of history?'

I had forgotten but I said yes and she went on. 'You should read a bit more history if you want to understand things better. It's full of the oddest damned things, you know. For example, India seems deeply connected to the letter M. You can start with Manu, come down to Maurya, Mughals, Mountbatten, Mohandas, Mohammad Ali, Shyama Prasad Mukherji, Morarji and so on. There's your statistician fellow also, Mahalanobis.'

I told her it would make quite a title for a book on potted biographies and she said the same thought had occurred to her and that she was planning to write one in her spare time.

'In fact,' she said, 'there is another odd thing that could be developed into a quickie, the fact that highly successful families last four generations. You can take any from history in any country and you will find that the decline begins when the fourth descendant takes over.'

It was nearly three-thirty by then and the waiters were hinting that we finish lunch and go. It was too late to go to the university now. Ms Bose said she would take a bus home and presently went off in search of one, leaving me at a loose end at a most awkward time. I went for a walk in the nearby park but got fed up of going round and round after a while and decided that I would go home, get into bed and read. It was that sort of day anyway, sunless and gloomy.

In the event, I didn't get into bed till well past midnight that day because when I reached home, I found Mike and Jyoti waiting for me on the verandah.

'Where have you been,' asked Jyoti. 'Your office said you had gone home at lunchtime.'

I asked them to come in and made some tea while they hung about in the kitchen grumbling to each other about a lot of things. I put the tray on the dining table, poured out the tea, fetched some biscuits, sat down and lit a cigarette.

The reason for their visit became apparent after they had argued a bit over which one of them was going to tell me why they had turned up unheralded. It was Jyoti who broke the news or rather asked the question.

'Can you move out of your flat to your club for a few days?'

'Two weeks or so, actually,' Mike mumbled.

I asked them why and they said there was a marriage in Jyoti's family and two of her uncles and aunts were refusing to stay in a hotel.

'They wanted to stay with us but we have only two bedrooms and Daddy and Mummy will stay there,' said Jyoti.

'We will pay your club charges,' Mike said.

I asked them when they wanted me to move out

and they said in about seven days. I thought for a bit about my resignation, my accumulated leave, the refusal of the company to let us cash it and agreed. I was getting pretty tired of that flat anyway and had been thinking of moving out. This seemed like a good opportunity to see if I really wanted to do that or whether I only needed a change from its sights and smells. But the idea of staying at the club didn't appeal to me very much, not for two weeks, anyway.

So, on the spur of the moment, I decided to visit Madhavi in the US. She was mopping up the crumbs around her thesis. Mike agreed to get me a complimentary ticket from his quota, subject to load, but with a stopover in London, hundred and twenty days return from date of departure. Jyoti said she would get the visa forms and fill them out so that all I had to do was to sign and deposit them at the US embassy.

All I needed to do now was to tell Nikki I was decamping for three months. I knew she would be very angry. I knew I was behaving very badly and that this was a violation of the tacit agreement we had reached that evening at her flat. I knew Ms Bose would be very disappointed with me and even Mrs Singhal, with her strong views on keeping your word, would disapprove strongly. I knew I was placing myself in the wrong with all of them. But when the need arose, I could be an absolute bastard, even if an imperfect one.

But somewhere deep within me there was this inexorable urge to leave it all behind. Books, publishing, the people in it, everything.

And that's what I did.